MY TOES ARE STARTING TO WIGGLE!

and other EASY Songs for Circle Time

BY "MISS JACKIE" WEISSMAN

Illustrated by Diane Foster

108 songs with circle time activities that develop motor, listening, language, cognitive, creative and self-esteem skills.

Thank you to the following contributors: Debra L. Berry, Mavis Bradford, Cindy Brown, Sharyn Connor, Marianne DeMarr, Barbara Elling, Misty Goosen, Ania Johnson, Valerie Krauss, Mary O. Lane, Sara McElhenny, Lynn Nelson, Elaine Raspel-Borth, Janet Reznicek, Marilyn Schugel, Emily Smith and Ruth Snowman.

© 1989 Jackie Weissman
Second Printing
ISBN 0-939514-12-5

Published by:
  Miss Jackie Music Company
  10001 El Monte
  Overland Park, Kansas 66207

Printed in the United States of America

Cover design and illustrations by Diane Foster

Editors:
  Ania Johnson
  Emily Smith

Distributed by:
  Gryphon House
  3706 Otis Street
  PO Box 211
  Mt. Ranier, Maryland 20822

FROM THE AUTHOR

This book has written itself over the past several years. It is an outgrowth of my teaching at the university, where teachers (my students) have shared their favorite "circle time" activities; it came from working with parents and finding out what songs their children love; and it grew out of doing what I like and do best: spending time with little children.

The songs and activities were carefully selected and are developmentally appropriate for children two to seven years old. Some are harder, some are easier, and you'll find you can use your judgment to adjust the songs and activities to fit your needs.

All the songs are musically sound, interesting and fun for children, and easy to learn and sing. (There is a cassette available, if you wish to listen to the melodies first.)

Music belongs in the lives of everyone, and any time a group of two or more gather, you'll find the songs and activities in this book are ones that you will sing again and again.

Miss Jackie

TABLE OF CONTENTS

SONG   JULY   PAGE

SONG   AUGUST   PAGE

A cassette tape of all the songs is available.

Write to:

MISS JACKIE MUSIC CO.
Department WT
10001 El Monte
Overland Park, KS 66207

SING A SONG OF SEPTEMBER

Words and Music by
"Miss Jackie" Weissman

Sing a song, sing a song of Sep-tem-ber.

Sing a song of the fal - ling leaves.

Sing a
1. friends and school and winds so cool.
2. birds and squir-rels and boys and girls.

Sing a song of Sep-tem - ber. Sing a-bout Sep-tem - ber.

Sing a sweet Sep-tem - ber song.

© 1981 Jackie Weissman
Recorded on *Sniggles, Squirrels and Chicken Pox, Vol. II*
Miss Jackie Music Co.

ACTIVITY

This song has a flowing, lilting feeling and suggests movement. Use a triangle or bell to accompany the song and have the children dance, jump, hop or skip as you sing the song.

Make a list of all the things associated with September and substitute those words in the two rhyming lines. Your words do not have to rhyme—the song is open-ended, and its purpose is to create a good feeling about September.

You can also sing the song about October, November and December by making up the appropriate words. For example: "Sing of witches and goblins and Halloween" or "Sing of Santa and presents and Christmas trees."

ADDITIONAL ACTIVITIES

• Take a nature walk and observe September: the changing colors of the leaves, the feel of the wind, the intensity of the sun.

• This is a good song for introducing the "s" sound. Pick out all the words in the song that start with "s" and discuss their meanings.

• Play this game: each time the children hear the "s" sound, they raise their hands (or wiggle a finger or shake a foot).

• Instead of "Sing a song," why not "Dance a song," "Jump a song," "Hop a song" or whatever other rhythm motor movement that your children can do?

FIVE CURRANT BUNS

Traditional

1. Five cur - rant buns in the bak - er's shop, Big and round with some su - gar on the top. A - long came Tom with a pen - ny to pay, Who bought a cur - rant bun and took it right a - way.

2. Four currant buns in the baker's shop . . .
3. Three currant buns in the baker's shop . . .
4. Two currant buns in the baker's shop . . .
5. One currant bun in the baker's shop . . .

Verse 6
No currant buns in the baker's shop,
Big and round with some sugar on the top.
No one came in with a penny to pay,
So close the baker's shop and have a baking day.

SKILLS: *Counting; creative dramatics.*

ACTIVITY

Explain to the children what a currant is: a kind of raisin, only smaller. Bring some currants and raisins to class to show the children what their differences are. Let them eat some of each so they can taste the difference.

Sing the song with the following motions:

Five currant buns	*(hold up five fingers)*
In the baker's shop	*(outline a house shape with your hands)*
Big and round	*(make a big circle with your hands)*
With some sugar on the top	*(pretend to sprinkle sugar with fingers)*
Along came Tom	*(make beckoning motion with hand)*
With a penny to pay	*(rub thumb and index finger together)*
Who bought a currant bun	*(hold out hand, palm up)*
And took it right away	*(bring hand into chest, fist closed)*

Repeat the song, holding up the appropriate number of fingers for each verse. Do the following motions for the last two lines of the last verse.

No one came	*(shake head)*
With a penny to pay	*(rub thumb and index finger together)*
So close the baker's shop	*(close palms together)*
And have a baking day	

ADDITIONAL ACTIVITY

• Act out the song. Choose five children to be "currant buns." Ask them to sit on the floor in a row.

Choose five other children to take away the "currant buns." Substitute the children's own names for "Tom."

Example:

Five currant buns in the baker's shop,
Big and round, with some sugar on the top.
Along came (*child's name*) with a penny to pay,
Who bought a currant bun and took it right away.

Each "taker" takes a "currant bun" out of the row until no "currant buns" are left. The "takers" then become the next "currant buns."

Have the rest of the class sing the song and do the motions while the others are acting it out. Let everyone have a turn at being the "currant buns" and the "takers."

This is a good activity to help the children learn each other's names.

OH WHEN THE BAND COMES MARCHING IN!

Traditional

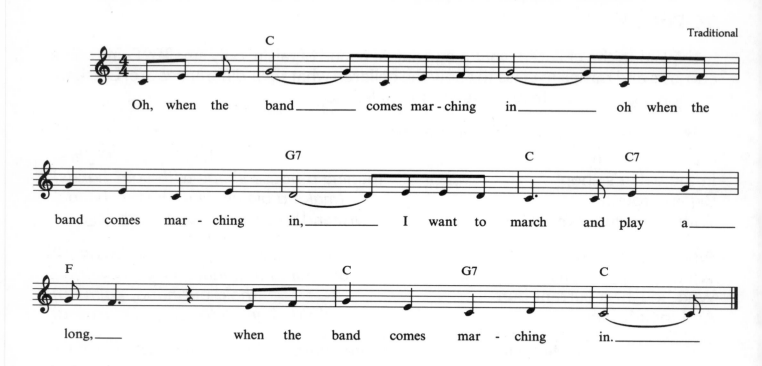

Oh, when the band_____ comes mar - ching in_____ oh when the

band comes mar - ching in,_____ I want to march and play a_____

long,_____ when the band comes mar - ching in._____

SKILL: *Develops listening skills*

"Circle time" can be a wonderful opportunity to teach your class about marching bands.

Oh When the Band Comes Marching In! is designed to go with the activities, but other songs may work as well. For instance, Sousa marches are perfect for these activities. Have plenty of rhythm instruments on hand to create your own marching band with your class.

ACTIVITY

After the children sit in a circle on the floor, give each child a rhythm instrument. Let them play along in time to the music as they sing the song, or have half the circle sing while the other half plays. (Switch parts so everyone gets a chance to play an instrument.)

ADDITIONAL ACTIVITIES

• Have the class stand up and march (single file) in the circle as they sing the song, then add the instruments.

This is a good time to teach them about marching bands—you might want to put on a recording of a march.

Have the children trade instruments so each child gets to play something different.

• Have the class sit in a circle on the floor. Divide the circle into groups by instruments—i.e., one group of woodblocks, one group of tambourines, etc.

The teacher is the "conductor." Direct the "band" by pointing to each group when you want them to play. Direct them to get louder by raising your arms gradually. Direct "softer" by lowering your arms. Tell the children ahead of time what each direction means.

Use for May Flowers dance.

OLD BRASS WAGON

American Folk Song

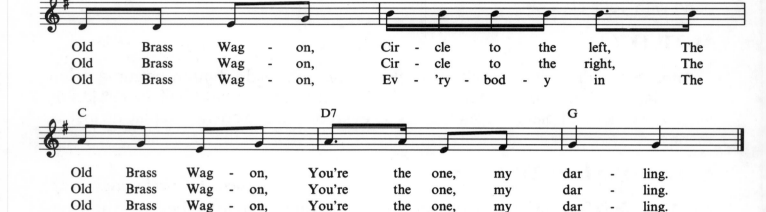

1. Cir-cle to the left, The Old Brass Wag-on, Cir-cle to the left, The
2. Cir-cle to the right, The Old Brass Wag-on, Cir-cle to the right, The
3. Ev-'ry-bod-y in The Old Brass Wag-on, Ev-'ry-bod-y in The

Old Brass Wag - on, Cir - cle to the left, The
Old Brass Wag - on, Cir - cle to the right, The
Old Brass Wag - on, Ev - 'ry - bod - y in The

Old Brass Wag - on, You're the one, my dar - ling.
Old Brass Wag - on, You're the one, my dar - ling.
Old Brass Wag - on, You're the one, my dar - ling.

4. Swing, oh swing, old brass wagon . . .
Partners link arms and swing

5. Promenade around, old brass wagon . . .
Partners walk around

6. Sashay up and down, old brass wagon . . .
Holding partner's hands, slide toward center of circle and out

7. Break and swing, old brass wagon . . .
Partners link arms and swing

8. Promenade home, old brass wagon . . .
Partners walk around

SKILLS: *Learning right-and-left concepts; group participation.*

ACTIVITY

Ask the children to form a circle. Teach the song a verse at a time so that the children can learn the dance steps. (Practice each movement before proceeding to the next verse.)

Circle to the left, the old brass wagon   *(join hands and circle to the left)*
Circle to the left, the old brass wagon
Circle to the left, the old brass wagon
You're the one, my darling   *(hug the person next to you)*

Circle to the right, the old brass wagon . . .   *(join hands and circle to the right)*

Everybody in, the old brass wagon . . .   *(join hands and move into the center of the circle)*

Everybody out, the old brass wagon . . .   *(move the circle back out)*

Everybody in, the old brass wagon . . .   *(move into the center of the circle)*

You're the one, my darling   *(hug the person next to you)*

ADDITIONAL ACTIVITIES

• Have the class sit in a circle on the floor. Change the words to include rhythmic motions they can do in place.

Clap your hands, the old brass wagon . . .   *(everyone claps hands)*

Tap your knees, the old brass wagon . . .   *(everyone taps knees with hands)*

• Variation: use rhythm sticks or other rhythm instruments to tap the rhythm while you sing the song.

FRIENDS

Adapted by
"MISS JACKIE" WEISSMAN

Smile a hap - py smile at ev - 'ry - one you meet,

Be a friend to them and you will see that

They'll smile back at you; Yes, they'll be your friends too.

SKILLS: *Language and social development.*

ACTIVITY

Have children stand facing a partner. Ask one of the partners to make a facial expression. The other partner should try to make the same facial expression.

Take turns making a face and being the "mirror."

ADDITIONAL ACTIVITIES

• Discuss how we can be friends—giving hugs, helping with a chore, holding hands, playing together, sharing.

Tell the children you're going to watch for people trying to be friends. Give the friends special stickers to wear. Give lots of praise to friendly behavior.

• Try smiling at people when they visit your room to see if they will smile back.

• Read *A Friend Is Someone Who Likes You,* by Joan Walsh Anglund.

• Cut pictures of friends out of magazines and glue them on a large paper letter "F." Explain to the children, " 'Friend' begins with the letter 'f.' " After the children have had time to look at the pictures, talk about the similarities they share.

Make an "experience chart," asking each child to complete this sentence: "A friend is _____." The teacher should record each child's response.

HEVENU SHALOM A'LEYCHEM

Israel: Greeting Song

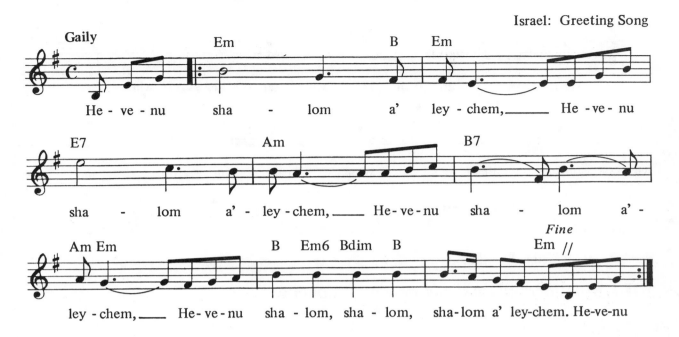

SKILL: *Learning "welcome" in a new language.*

ACTIVITY

This song is an Israeli greeting song. The word "shalom" has three meanings: hello, goodbye, and peace.

Have the children form a circle. Teach them the song and let them march while they sing it. They should sing the song enthusiastically, with the last two "shaloms" SHOUTED out. Have each child take a partner, clasp hands and march around the circle together as they sing the song.

ADDITIONAL ACTIVITIES

• Use this song at the start of the class.

• Sing it while waiting in line, traveling on the bus, etc.

• Instead of marching around the circle, let the children stand in place and stomp their feet or clap their hands while they sing.

NOTE: Since "shalom" also means "goodbye," this song will work just as well at the end of the day as the beginning.

THE SEASONS

SKILLS: *Vocabulary development; creativity.*

ACTIVITY

Sing the song and ask the children to name all the things they can do during each season. For example, "What can you do in the wintertime?" might elicit responses such as "ride sleds," "ice skate," etc. Springtime could include "planting seeds" or "picking flowers," summertime "drinking lemonade" or "swimming," autumntime "raking leaves" or "carving pumpkins."

Change the words to "What do you like in the _____ 'time?" and sing about the things that the class likes about each season.

ADDITIONAL ACTIVITIES

* Try changing the verses to see what other responses you get. Examples:

What do you eat when you are hungry?
What do you see when you watch TV?
What can you do on a rainy day?
What can you do at a birthday party?
What can you do at school?

* Ask a child to stand in the center of the circle. After telling where or when it happens, ask the child to pantomime one of the actions sung about.

TEACHER: What can you do at school?
CHILD: Draw pictures, sing a song, read a book.

The child in the middle of the circle pantomimes one of the activities, such as drawing a picture. The rest of the class must guess what the child is doing.

Make sure everyone has a chance to pantomime. (Note: this is an excellent rainy day activity!)

GREETING SONG
(Are You Sleeping?)

French Folk Song

Where is Lar - ry? Where is Lar - ry? Here I am!

Here I am! How are you to - day, sir? (miss)

Ver - y well, I thank you. Glad you're here! Glad you're here!

SKILLS: *Develop listening skills; taking turns.*

ACTIVITY

Teach the song to the children, then use it as a greeting when they come into the classroom at the beginning of the day.

Example:

TEACHER: Where is ("Larry")? Where is Larry?
CHILD: Here I am! Here I am!
TEACHER: How are you today, sir?
CHILD: Very well, I thank you.
TEACHER: Glad you're here! Glad you're here!

Or, have everyone sit in a circle when they first come in. Sing the song and ask each child to raise a hand when hearing his or her name called. (This is a fun way to take attendance!)

ADDITIONAL ACTIVITY

• Have the children sit in a circle and give each of them a rhythm instrument to play. Ask them to wait until it is their turn.

Sing the verse, but instead of having the child answer "Here I am!" ask that the instrument be played in response. (Note: this works well with children who have delayed speech.)

HOW DO YOU DO?

Source Unknown

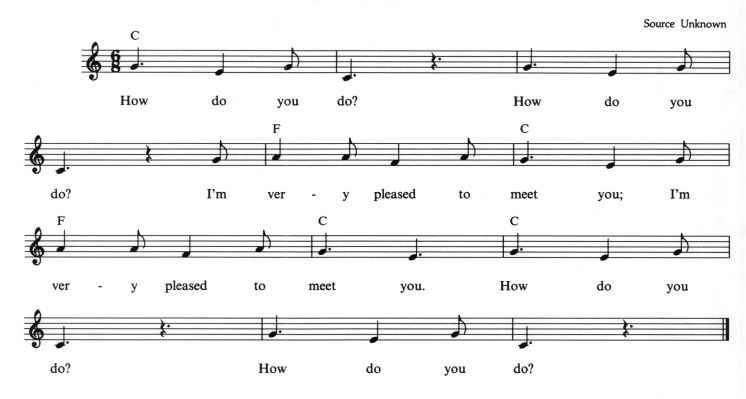

SKILL: *A great way to learn names.*

ACTIVITY

Have each child stand facing a partner. Make a circle of the sets of partners (some face in while others face out). The children sing the song and do the following motions.

How do you do?	*(children bow or curtsy to partner)*
How do you do?	
I'm very pleased to meet you	*(children shake hands with partner)*
I'm very pleased to meet you	
How do you do?	*(children bow or curtsy to partner)*
How do you do?	

Have each child say his or her name, then move to a new partner. (An easy way to change partners: have one circle remain still while the other moves one step to the side.)

ADDITIONAL ACTIVITY

• For a variation on the song, substitute "My name is (John)" for the last line of the song. This way, children sing rather than say their names at the end. Have the children sit in a circle on the floor to sing the song. Point to each one in turn to sing their names.

GO ROUND AND ROUND THE VILLAGE

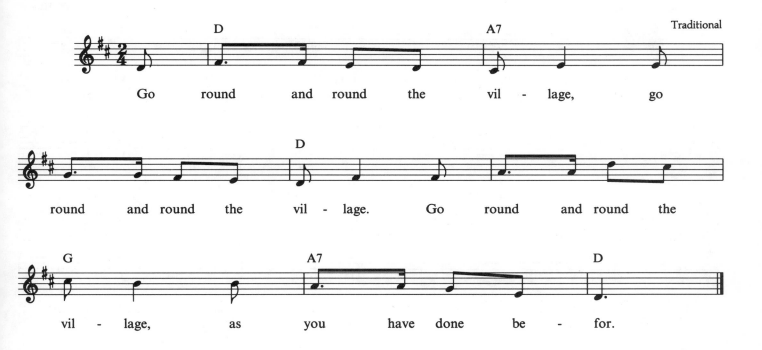

Go round and round the vil - lage, go round and round the vil - lage. Go round and round the vil - lage, as you have done be - for.

SKILL: *Enjoyment of a singing game.*

ACTIVITY

Select one child to wear a witch's hat and ride a broomstick. Sing, "Witch goes round the village, witch goes round the village, witch goes round the village as she/he has done before."

The "witch" walks in and out of the children in the circle. As the "witch" touches the children, they raise their hands high in the air. At the end of the song, the "witch," with closed eyes, points to a new "witch" and the game begins again.

ADDITIONAL ACTIVITY

• Play this game using the children's names or other characters and props—a fire-fighter's hat, an astronaut's helmet, etc. Adapt the words to fit the character.

HALLOWEEN IS COMING

Traditional

Hal - lo - ween is com - ing, Ha, Ha, Ha! Hal - lo - ween is

com - ing, Ha, Ha, Ha! Spooks will prowl on Hal - lo - ween;

Bats and gob - lins will soon be seen; Ghosts will float right

through the air; Wit - ches on broom - sticks will give you a scare.

SKILLS: *Developing listening, language and motor skills.*

ACTIVITY

Ask the children to form a circle. Do the following actions while singing the song.

Halloween is coming, ha, ha, ha! *(creep spookily around the circle on tiptoe)*
Halloween is coming, ha, ha, ha!

Spooks will prowl on Halloween *(creep around the circle on tiptoe; make a spooky face)*

Bats and goblins will soon be seen *(flap arms like wings; show your fangs)*

Ghosts will float right through the air *(wave your arms all around; be careful not to bump into any other "ghosts")*

Witches on broomsticks will give you a scare *(pretend to ride on a broomstick; gallop around the circle)*

ADDITIONAL ACTIVITIES

• Make spooky puppets by painting popsicle sticks to look like witches, ghosts, bats, etc. Act out the song using the puppets.

• Make Halloween masks out of paper bags or construction paper for the class to wear. (If using paper bags, make sure the holes for eyes, nose and mouth are large enough for good ventilation.) Let the class wear the masks while they sing and act out the song.

FIVE LITTLE PUMPKINS

Unknown

Five lit - tle pump - kins sit - ting on a gate, The first one said, "Oh

my, it's get - ting late." The sec - ond one said, "There are wit - ches in the air." The

third one said, "But we don't care." The fourth one said, "Let's run and run and run." The

fifth one said, "I'm read - y for some fun." "Oo - oo!" went the wind and

out went the light, And the five lit - tle pump - kins rolled___ out of sight.

SKILL: *Developing counting skills.*

ACTIVITY

Hold up five fingers ("pumpkins").

First "pumpkin"	*Point one finger to your wrist*
Second "pumpkin"	*Wave both hands in the air over your head*
Third "pumpkin"	*Flop both hands forward, bending at the wrists*
Fourth "pumpkin"	*Make fists and move them in circles beside your body (as though running)*
Fifth "pumpkin"	*Point thumbs toward chest*
"Oo-oo"	*Throw arms up in air*
"Out"	*Clap hands in front of your body*
"And"	*Hands make a rolling motion away from your body*

ADDITIONAL ACTIVITY

• Have five children sit in a row on the floor. Give each a number from one to five.

The rest of the class sings the song while the "pumpkins" do the actions—pumpkin number one points to wrist, pumpkin number two waves both hands in the air, etc. All of the pumpkins do the motions for the first line of the song and the last two lines, starting with "oo-oo."

Give each child a chance to be a pumpkin.

WHAT DO YOU LIKE ABOUT HALLOWEEN?

Words & Music
Miss Jackie Weissman

What do you like a - bout Hal - lo - ween?

What do you like a - bout Hal - lo - ween?

Solo: I like the (ghosts). *Group:* He likes the (ghosts).

Group: That's what we like a - bout Hal - lo - ween.

©1980 Jackie Weissman

SKILLS: *Sequencing; listening.*

ACTIVITY

Halloween is an exciting holiday for children. Ask the children what ideas Halloween brings to mind. You will probably get these answers: "witches," "ghosts," "monsters," "bats," "black cats," "costumes" and "trick-or-treat."

Everyone sings the song "What Do You Like About Halloween?" One child sings, "I like the _____," (for example, "ghosts"). Then, everyone sings together, "He likes the ghosts. That's what we like about Halloween."

Now pick a second child, who sings, "I like the _____ ," (for example, "witch"). The class echoes, "She likes the witch." After the second child and the class have sung their parts, the first child sings his part again.

Pick a third child and proceed as above. With each succeeding verse, add a solo part. You'll soon have a children's version of Gilbert and Sullivan in your own classroom!

ADDITIONAL ACTIVITIES

• After the children learn their parts and how to sing the song, substitute sounds for the names of the characters. Sing, "I like the *(make sound)*." The children repeat, "She likes the *(make sound)*."

• Make up other versions for other holidays. This song can be used year-round.

CHRISTOPHER COLUMBUS

Words and music by
"MISS JACKIE" WEISSMAN

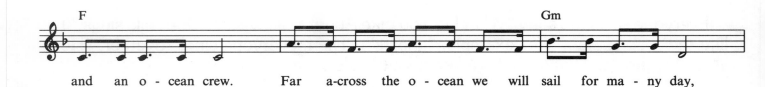

I'm Chris-to-pher Co-lum-bus, I sail the o-cean blue,__ I have three ships to take a-long

and an o-cean crew. Far a-cross the o-cean we will sail for ma-ny day,

We are look-ing for A-mer-i-ca._____ A-hoy!_____ A-

hoy! We are look-ing for A-mer-i-ca.

©1988 JACKIE WEISSMAN

SKILL: *Learning about Christopher Columbus.*

ACTIVITY

Have the children sit in a circle on the floor. Ask one child to be "Christopher Columbus" and walk around the outside of the circle "looking for America." (Note: child may shade eyes as if looking for something while walking around the circle.)

The rest of the class sings the song. At its end, whoever "Christopher Columbus" is standing behind becomes the next "Christopher Columbus."

ADDITIONAL ACTIVITIES

• Explain to the children that Christopher Columbus is credited with being the first European to discover America, thereby opening the way for others to settle the new land.

Teach the song to the children after you tell them the story of the voyage. Point out that his ships first sighted land on October 12, 1492, and that is why we celebrate Columbus Day in October.

• If possible, bring a large map of the world to class (or use a globe). Show the children where Spain is, the country where Columbus began his journey.

Trace the voyage on the map across the Atlantic Ocean to San Salvador, where Columbus first landed. Show where the United States is so they can see how far from this country the explorer first sighted land.

• Act out the story of Columbus with the class.

Write the ships' names—the Nina, Pinta and Santa Maria—on three large pieces of posterboard. Choose three children to be "ships" and hold up the ship names.

Choose a "Columbus," and divide the rest of the class into "crew" and "Indians." Put the "Indians" on one side of the classroom, "Columbus" and the "crew" on the other. Let the groups slowly move to the other sides of the room while everyone sings the song.

SIX LITTLE MICE

English Folk Song

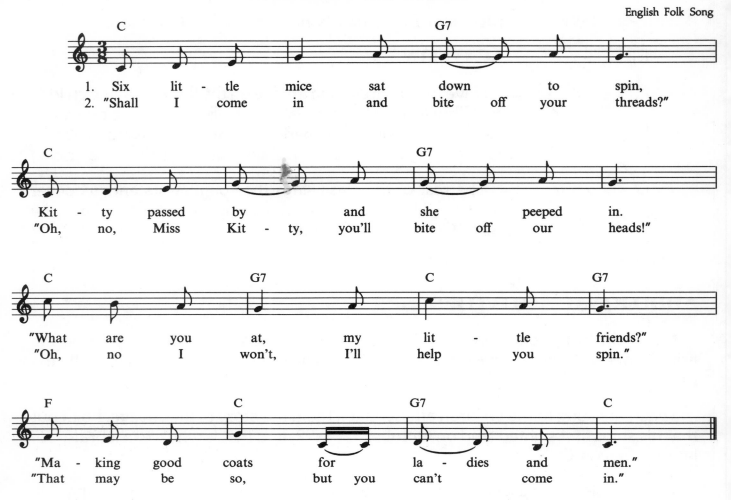

1. Six lit - tle mice sat down to spin,
2. "Shall I come in and bite off your threads?"

Kit - ty passed by and she peeped in.
"Oh, no, Miss Kit - ty, you'll bite off our heads!"

"What are you at, my lit - tle friends?"
"Oh, no I won't, I'll help you spin."

"Ma - king good coats for la - dies and men."
"That may be so, but you can't come in."

SKILLS: *Language development; listening skills; dramatic play.*

ACTIVITY

Here is a fingerplay to do with this delightful English folk song.

Six little mice sat down to spin   *(roll hands)*
Kitty passed by and she peeped in   *(peek through hands)*
What are you at, my little friends?
Making good coats for ladies and men   *(sewing with needle and thread)*

Shall I come in and bite off your threads?   *(hands on hips and bite with mouth)*
Oh no, Miss Kitty, you'll bite off our heads!   *(shake head and finger and point to head)*

Oh no, I won't. I'll help you spin   *(shake head "no" and roll hands)*

That may be so, but you can't come in!   *(shake finger at "cat")*

ADDITIONAL ACTIVITIES

• Make a dramatic play using the song.

Make headbands with the appropriate ears—some with mouse ears, some with cat ears—for the children to wear. Pair up six mice with six cats. Sing the song, then have each pair trade headbands so that each child gets to sing each part.

You may need to run through the play several times so everyone in the class has a chance to participate.

• Find a picture of a spinning wheel in a book or encyclopedia. Explain to the class how it was used a long time ago to make cloth and to sew with.

How is a spinning wheel different from a modern sewing machine? Do any of the children have sewing machines at home? How do they work?

JACK-O'-LANTERN SONG

Moderately

Source Unknown

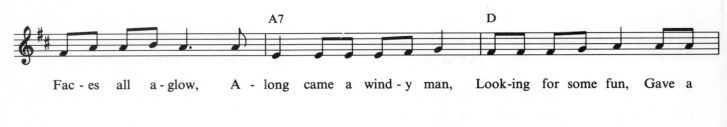

Five lit-tle Jack O' Lan-terns, sit-ting in a row,___ Five lit-tle Jack O' Lan-terns,

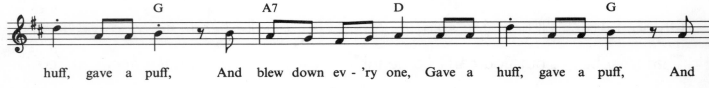

Fac-es all a-glow, A-long came a wind-y man, Look-ing for some fun, Gave a

huff, gave a puff, And blew down ev-'ry one, Gave a huff, gave a puff, And

A7 D **Ritardando** G D A7 D

blew down ev-'ry one,___ Naugh-ty Mis-ter Wind-y Man, Blew down ev-'ry one.___

SKILLS: *Counting; creative dramatics.*

ACTIVITY

Choose five children to be the jack-o'-lanterns. Have them sit in a row on the floor. The rest of the class sings the song while holding up five fingers.

When the words "Gave a huff, gave a puff" are sung, the five jack-o'-lanterns fall to the ground. On "Naughty Mr. Windy Man," the children shake their index fingers as if reprimanding someone.

ADDITIONAL ACTIVITIES

• Choose one child to be "Mr. Windy Man." In the "huff" and "puff" part of the song, "Mr. Windy" gets to make the sounds.

• Let the children decorate pumpkin patterns and hold them up as the song is sung.

• Think of other things the jack-o'-lantern could do: run, hop, skip, etc. Make use of developing motor skills.

GO TELL AUNT RHODY

Traditional

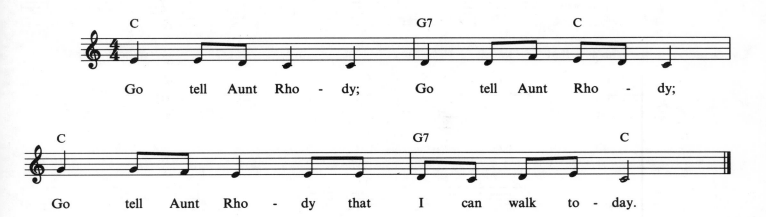

Go tell Aunt Rho - dy; Go tell Aunt Rho - dy;

Go tell Aunt Rho - dy that I can walk to - day.

SKILLS: *Large muscle development; self-esteem.*

ACTIVITY

Have the class walk around the circle while singing the song. Ask one child to select another movement to do while singing the song: jumping, hopping, skipping, etc.

ADDITIONAL ACTIVITIES

• Ask the class what kinds of movements can be done in place. For instance, they can touch their toes, wiggle all over, etc. Sing the song again, using these actions.

• Change "Aunt Rhody" to a child's name and sing something positive about that child.

Go tell Billy,
Go tell Billy,
Go tell Billy
He has a nice smile.

Ask the children what they like about Billy and sing it. Do this with each child, letting the class say something nice.

WHO'S THAT KNOCKING?

SKILLS: *Vocabulary development; listening skills.*

ACTIVITY

Make a "door" large enough for a child to hide behind out of posterboard or a large piece of cardboard. Draw a doorknob on it to make it look more real.

Choose one child to be the first "hider," standing behind the door with eyes closed. Choose another child to "visit."

The "visitor" should make a sound such as laughing, coughing, barking, etc. The class then sings the song, substituting the sound the child made for the word "knock-ing."

Who's that *(laughing sounds)* at my door?
Who's that *(laughing sounds)* at my door?
Who's that *(laughing sounds)* at my door?

The child behind the door must guess who the "visitor" is. The "visitor" then takes a turn hiding behind the door.

Play the game until each child has had a turn at being both "hider" and "visitor."

ADDITIONAL ACTIVITY

• Have the class sit in a circle on the floor. Let the children pretend to knock with their fists in the air as they sing.

Point to a child on the last line. The rest of the class sings, "It is (Paula)." Continue the song until each child's name has been sung.

This is a good icebreaker for the beginning of the year or when a new child comes into the class—it helps the children learn each other's names.

TURKEY TALK

Words and Music by
"Miss Jackie" Weissman

Well Hel - lo Mis - ter Tur - key tell me what do you say as you

stand in the yard and watch the chil - dren at play Spread your

wings Mis - ter Tur - key stretch your neck high and tall Talk to

me Mis - ter Tur - key tell me a - ny - thing at all.

SKILLS: *Listening; language; creative dramatics.*

ACTIVITY

This song gives children the opportunity to explore sound in many different ways.

What does a turkey's voice sound like—is it high? low? loud? soft? fast? slow?

How does a turkey say "hello"? How does a turkey say "I want to play"? Have the children talk to each other using "turkey talk."

ADDITIONAL ACTIVITIES

• **Listening skills**—Tell the children a story. Every time they hear the word "turkey," they make "turkey talk."

• **Dramatic play**—Make turkey masks from paper bags or wear a turkey picture as you sing the song.

• **Language**—Make up a sentence and substitute "turkey" for one of the words. Let the children guess what the substituted word is.

• **Identification**—If possible, make a field trip to see a real turkey. Discuss the ways that various birds fly.

A PUMPKIN RAN AWAY

Source Unknown

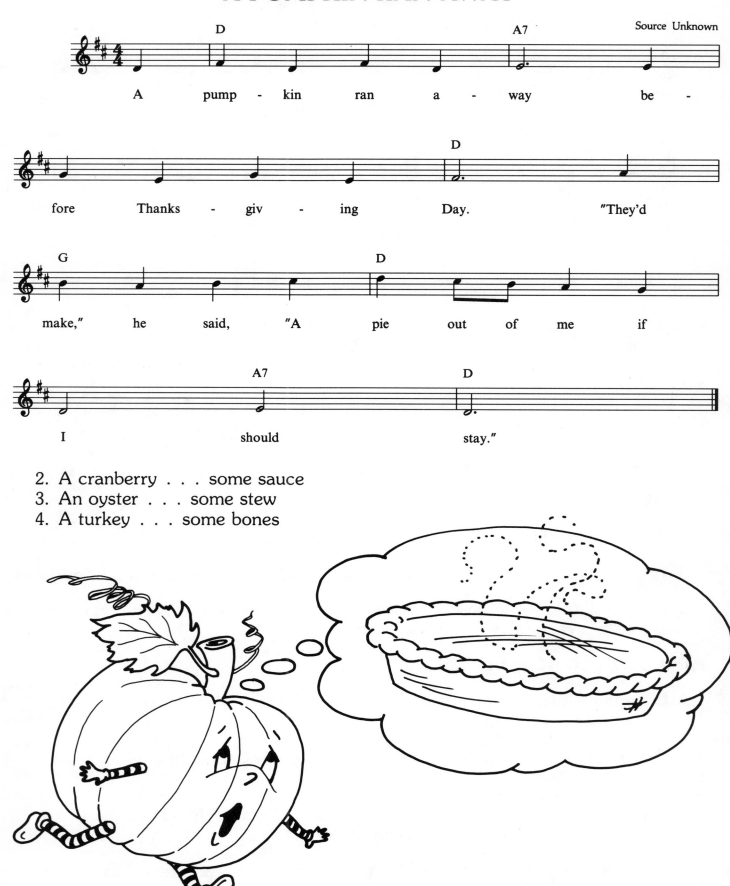

A pump - kin ran a - way be -

fore Thanks - giv - ing Day. "They'd

make," he said, "A pie out of me if

I should stay."

2. A cranberry . . . some sauce
3. An oyster . . . some stew
4. A turkey . . . some bones

SKILL: *Learning about holiday traditions.*

ACTIVITY

Sing the song through with the children. Ask them what other foods they eat at Thanksgiving—their answers may surprise you!

Make up verses for the song using the children's ideas. Examples:

A green bean ran away . . . "They'd make," he said, "a casserole out of me"

Chocolate—some fudge

Peanut butter—a sandwich

Pecan—a pie

ADDITIONAL ACTIVITY

• This song is easily adapted to other holidays. The following example is for a Fourth of July picnic.

A chicken ran away before Independence Day.
"They'd make," she said, "barbecue out of me if I should stay."

Potato—some chips

Watermelon—some seeds

Ice cream—a sundae

The possibilities are virtually limitless. Make up verses for other holidays—Easter, Christmas, Hannukah, Valentine's Day, etc.

FIVE LITTLE CHICKADEES

Singing Game

1. Five lit - tle chick - a - dees peep - ing at the door,
2. Four lit - tle chick - a - dees sit - ting in a tree,

One flew a - way, and then there were four.
One flew a - way, and then there were three.

Chorus

Chick - a - dee, chick - a - dee, hap - py and gay,

Chick - a - dee, chick - a - dee, fly a - way.

3. Three little chickadees looking at you,
   One flew away, and then there were two

4. Two little chickadees sitting in the sun,
   One flew away, and then there was one.

5. One little chickadee left all alone,

   It flew away, and then there was none.

SKILLS: *Counting; memory; language development; dramatic play.*

ACTIVITY

This is a flannel board story. You'll need a door, a tree, a sun and five chickadees *(see pattern on pages 185 and 186)*. You will also need cards numbering zero to five.

After the children have learned the song, set up the flannel board with the door, sun and tree. Hold up the card with number five. Ask a child to put five chickadees in the tree.

The class counts together—"one, two, three, four, five." Everyone sings the song and when the words say "chickadee fly away," the same child removes one of the birds. The class then counts the chickadees again—"one, two, three, four."

Take off all the birds and choose another child to come and put up four chickadees. Repeat the same activity.

After it's learned, this circle-time game can be played without the direction of a teacher. Set it up at a learning center and let the children do it on their own.

ADDITIONAL ACTIVITIES

• Play the game using fingers for the chickadees. "Fly" hand behind back.

• Let the children be "chickadees" and "fly away" in the song.

• Substitute other animal names for "chickadees" (lions, bears, turtles, etc.). Let the children move like each new animal.

OLD MACDONALD

Traditional

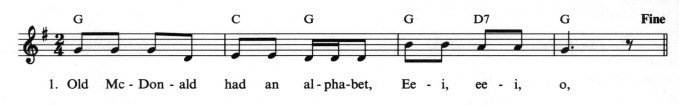

1. Old Mc-Don-ald had an al-pha-bet, Ee - i, ee - i, o,

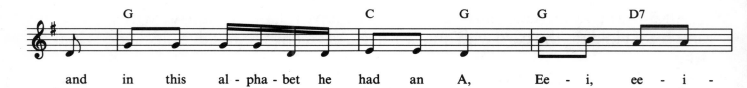

and in this al-pha-bet he had an A, Ee - i, ee - i -

o, with an A A here, and an A A there,

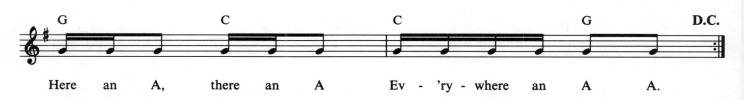

Here an A, there an A Ev - 'ry - where an A A.

SKILLS: *Listening; sentence memory; letter recognition.*

ACTIVITY

Sing the song with this new verse to help the class learn letters.

Old MacDonald had an alphabet. E I E I O.
And in this alphabet he had an A. E I E I O.
With an A, A here and an A, A there,
Here an A, there an A, everywhere an A, A.
Old MacDonald had an alphabet. E I E I O.

Put cards with the letters of the alphabet in a bag or box. Let each child have a turn at picking a letter.

The child holds up the letter and the rest of the class sings the song about that particular letter. (The child holding the letter can raise it up each time the letter is named in the song.)

ADDITIONAL ACTIVITIES

- Change the verses to include numbers or colors. For example:

Old MacDonald had a number. E I E I O.
And with this number he had a TWO. E I E I O.

Old MacDonald had a color. E I E I O.
And in this color he had a GREEN. E I E I O.

Change the cards in the box to show numbers or colors.

- Sing the song with the traditional verses and sign the animals.

farm
Five shape RH palm in, tips left. Place thumb on left side of chin and draw across to right side.

horse
H shape RH thumb extended. Place thumb on right temple. Flap H fingers downward twice.

pig
Place back of RH, fingers together, under chin. Flap tips down once.

chicken
Place side of right G on mouth then place tips in left palm.

pony
P shape RH. Place thumb knuckle of right P on right temple. Twist middle finger forward and down twice.

cow
Place thumb of right Y on right temple and twist forward.

duck
Snap thumb and index and middle fingers together at mouth (to indicate duck quacking).

rooster
Three shape RH palm left. Tap forehead with thumb twice.

sheep
Clip together tips of right V, palm up, on left forearm (as if clipping wool). Repeat motion.

goat
Flick tips of right bent V on chin then on forehead.

turkey
Place back of right Q on tip of nose then shake down in front of chest.

goose
LH open B palm down, tips right. G shape RH. Rest right elbow on back of left hand.

FIVE FAT TURKEYS

Traditional

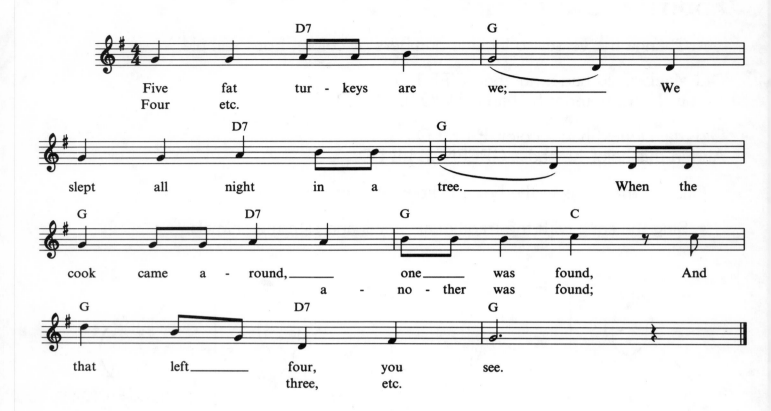

SKILLS: *Cognitive; learning numbers; creative dramatics.*

ACTIVITY

Choose five children to be "turkeys." Have them sit on a pretend tree. Choose another child to be "cook."

While the rest of the class sings the song, "cook" takes one "turkey" from the "tree" for each verse.

ADDITIONAL ACTIVITY

• Here's a fingerplay for this song.

Five fat turkeys are we	*(hold hand up and wiggle fingers)*
We slept all night in a tree	*(fold fingers over palm)*
When the cook came around	*(make a fist with the other hand;*
	act as though you are shaking a salt shaker)
One was found	*(point one finger in the air)*
And that left four, you see	*(fold down thumb of "turkey" hand)*

Repeat all of the above actions for each verse, but keep fingers of "turkey" hand folded down as you count down in the song.

Point to the window,
Point to the door, Up to the
ceil - ing, Down to the floor.

SKILLS: *Listening; following directions.*

ACTIVITY

Use a puppet (such as "Bert," of Jim Henson's Muppets) to demonstrate how to point.

Sing the song through once for the children, then say the words to the song while using the puppet to point. Do this one verse at a time.

Have the children do the following actions with the teacher and the puppet as they sing the song.

Point to the window   *(point to the window)*
Point to the door   *(point to the door)*
Up to the ceiling   *(point to the ceiling)*
Down to the floor   *(point to the floor)*

Add other verses, such as "Point to a table, point to a chair, point to a friend *good* of yours sitting over there" or "Point to your head now, point to your knee, point to your elbow, now point to me."

This song provides nonverbal children with an excellent opportunity to communicate.

ADDITIONAL ACTIVITIES

• Let the children take turns using the puppet to point to things. Or make puppets out of popsicle sticks for the children to point with.

Call out an object in the room. Ask the children to point to it without speaking.

• Change the verses to include the children's names—"Point to Jimmy, point to Susie, point to Mary, point to Bobby." Ask everyone to point to the child being named in the song. (This is a good way to help them learn each other's names.)

WHAT ARE YOU WEARING?

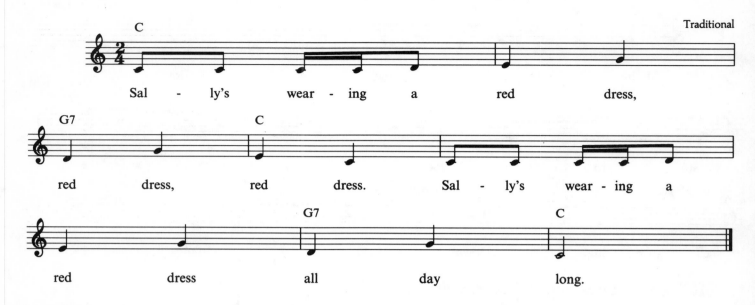

Traditional

Sal - ly's wear - ing a red dress, red dress, red dress. Sal - ly's wear - ing a red dress all day long.

SKILLS: *Learning about colors; self-concept; language development; developing awareness of others.*

ACTIVITY

Have the children sit in a circle on the floor. The teacher begins the song.

TEACHER: I am wearing a *(red dress)*, *(red dress)*, *(red dress)*.
I am wearing a *(red dress)* all day long.

CHILDREN: Teacher's wearing a *(red dress)*, *(red dress)*, *(red dress)*.
Teacher's wearing a *(red dress)* all day long.

Go around the circle, letting each child choose one article of clothing he/she is wearing. Let the child sing about the clothing, then have the class repeat the verse. This will reinforce color and clothing awareness. (Note: if a child is too shy to sing about himself/herself, sing along with the child.)

ADDITIONAL ACTIVITY

• Change the words of the song to teach other concepts. For example, "Jimmy's wearing a happy face," etc.

AT THE TELEPHONE

Hungarian Folk Song

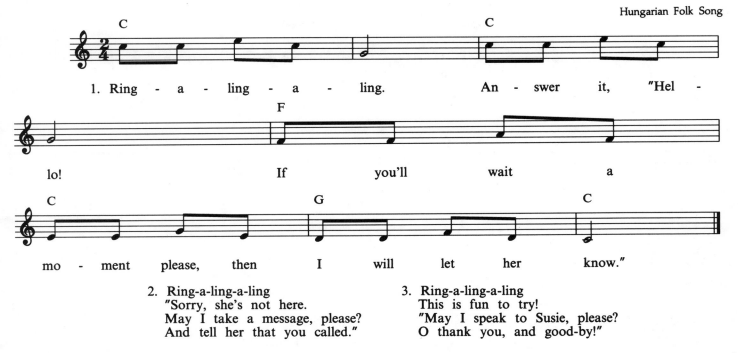

1. Ring - a - ling - a - ling. An - swer it, "Hel -
lo! If you'll wait a
mo - ment please, then I will let her know."

2. Ring-a-ling-a-ling
"Sorry, she's not here.
May I take a message, please?
And tell her that you called."

3. Ring-a-ling-a-ling
This is fun to try!
"May I speak to Susie, please?
O thank you, and good-by!"

SKILLS: *Learning to use the telephone and take messages.*

ACTIVITY

Teach the children about telephone manners before teaching the song. Then, sing the song together and do the following actions.

Ring-a-ling-a-ling
Answer it, "Hello!"
If you'll wait a moment, please,
Then I will let her know.

(one child "rings," using triangle)
(another child "answers,"
puts a hand over the mouthpiece,
then calls someone)

Ring-a-ling-a-ling
Sorry, she's not here.
May I take a message, please,
And tell her that you called?

(one child "rings," using triangle)
(answering child shakes head)
(the child picks up pencil and paper
and pretends to write a message)

Ring-a-ling-a-ling
This is fun to try!
May I speak to Susie, please?
Oh, thank you, and goodbye!

(one child pretends to dial a number)
(the child pretends to converse)
(the child hangs up the phone)

ADDITIONAL ACTIVITY

• Ask the children what number to call in case of emergencies. Let them practice dialing the number on a toy phone.

Review with the children their home phone numbers. They can practice dialing those numbers on the toy phone, also.

MARY WORE A RED DRESS

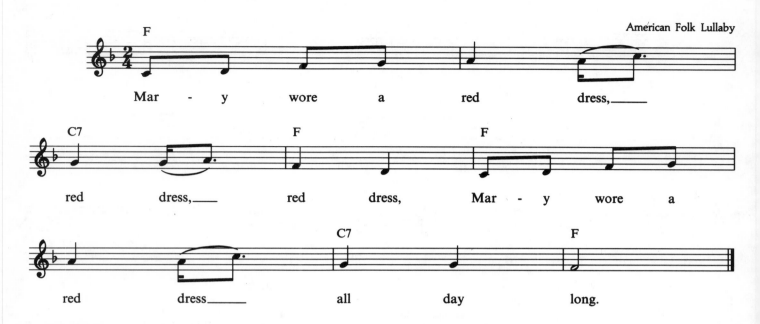

American Folk Lullaby

Mar - y wore a red dress,____
red dress,____ red dress, Mar - y wore a
red dress____ all day long.

SKILLS: *Listening skills; color concepts; vocabulary.*

ACTIVITY

Sing the song with the children using a child's name and color of clothing. For example: "Billy wore a blue shirt," etc.

Once the children have learned the song, let each child stand up and be sung about. You can sing about any article of clothing.

ADDITIONAL ACTIVITY

• Make birds out of construction paper and attach them to headbands made of tagboard strips. Pass out the headbands, then sing about each of the birds.

Johnny is a red bird, red bird, red bird.
Johnny is a red bird all day long.

Johnny can "fly" around the room like a bird while the rest of the class sings.

AFRICAN NOEL

Liberian Folk Song

SKILLS: *Movement game; "soft" and "loud" concepts.*

ACTIVITY

Have the children stand in a circle. Everyone step-slides to the right on the first line and claps on the last note of the line. Step-slide to the left on the second line, clapping on the last note of the line. Join hands and walk toward the center of the circle while singing "Sing we all noel," four steps in and four steps out again. Repeat step-slides on the last two lines.

ADDITIONAL ACTIVITIES

• Have on hand some rhythm instruments such as wooden blocks, sticks and maracas. Let half the class play the instruments in time to the song as the other half sings, then switch so that everyone gets a chance to play the instruments.

• Have the class sing the first two lines *pianissimo* (softly) and the middle two lines *forte* (loudly). Sing the last two lines softly.

HANUKKAH

Jewish Folk Song

Adapted
Miss Jackie Weissman

Han - uk - kah,   Han - uk - kah,   hap - py   hol - i -   day.

Chil - dren sing,   chil - dren dance,   can - dles   burn a -   way.

Han - uk - kah,   Han - uk - kah,   tops spin 'round and 'round.

Spin spin spin   spin spin spin   what a   love - ly   sound.

SKILL: *Learning about a Jewish holiday.*

ACTIVITY

Hanukkah is a celebration of the defeat of the Syrian Army by Judah Maccabee in the year 165 B.C. This defeat gave the Jews freedom to worship as they believed and to rebuild their temple in Jerusalem. Hanukkah is meaningful to all people because it represents freedom.

The holiday is celebrated for eight days to commemorate the "miracle" of the eternal light—though the people of Jerusalem thought there was only enough oil to burn in the temple for one day, it burned a full eight. During the holiday people give presents, eat special foods and hold parties.

This song is lovely to use rhythm instruments with. At the end of every four measures is a pause where triangles, tone blocks and tambourines sound wonderful.

> Hanukkah, Hanukkah, happy holiday. *(Play the instruments one beat)*
> *Children sing, children dance,*
> *Candles blaze away. (Instruments, etc.)*

On the words "Hanukkah, Hanukkah," the children pretend to be tops* and spin around and around. On the words 'Spin, spin, spin, spin, spin, what a lovely sound," the children make a *whooosh* sound with their voices and fall to the ground.

ADDITIONAL ACTIVITY

• Divide the group into two parts. One part sings the song and plays the instruments, the other group can be the tops.

* The Hebrew word for "top" is dreydel.

MISS POLLY HAD A DOLLY

Unknown

SKILLS: *Rhyming words; having fun.*

ACTIVITY

Do the following fingerplay with this song.

Miss Polly had a dolly who was sick, sick, sick   *(rock baby)*
She sent for the doctor to come quick, quick, quick   *(pretend to call doctor*
                                                       on telephone)
The doctor came with his bag and his hat   *(pretend to hold bag with one hand,*
                                                      take off hat with the other)

And he knocked on the door with a rat-a-tat-tat *(pretend to knock on door)*

The doctor looked at Dolly and he shook his head *(shake head)*
Told Miss Polly, "Put her straight to bed" *(lay head on hands as though sleeping)*
He wrote out a paper for a pill, pill, pill *(pretend to write on hand)*
"I'll be back in the morning with my bill, bill, bill" *(hold hand out, palm up)*

ADDITIONAL ACTIVITIES

• Act out the song with the class.

Bring a doll to class to be "Dolly." Ask one child to be "Miss Polly," another to be "Doctor." Give "Doctor" a toy medical bag or a handbag. Have "actors" do the motions while the rest of the class sings the song.

Other props to have ready: a toy telephone, a doll bed (to put "Dolly" into), a cardboard door with a doorknob painted on and a piece of paper for the prescription.

• Use this song as an opportunity to talk about healthy habits.

Ask the children why they think "Dolly" is sick. What could be done to keep from getting sick? Help them get started thinking. Mention things like dressing warmly in cold weather, eating plenty of good foods like vegetables and fruit, getting plenty of rest, etc.

I'M TALL, I'M SMALL

Unknown

Bb

I'm tall, I'm ver - y tall. I'm

F7   **Bb**   **Bb**

small, I'm ver - y small. Some - times I'm tall, some -

F7   **Bb**

times I'm small. Guess what I am now.

SKILLS: *Listening skills; vocabulary development; the concep* *"small."*

ACTIVITY

Ask the children to stand in a circle. Sing the song and do the following motions.

I'm tall, I'm very tall	*(everyone stands up as straight as possible)*
I'm small, I'm very small	*(everyone squats down on the floor)*
Sometimes I'm tall	*(stand up straight)*
Sometimes I'm small	*(squat on floor)*
Guess what I am now!	*(leave it up to the children—*
	each child either stands tall or squats)

ADDITIONAL ACTIVITIES

• By changing the words of the song slightly, it can be used to work on number recognition, colors or the alphabet.

Have colored cards on hand or put letters or numbers on 3"x5" cards. Give each child a card. Sing the song and have the child with the appropriate card hold it up when the color (or number or letter) is mentioned in the song.

I'm blue	*(child with blue card holds it up)*
I am yellow	*(child with yellow card holds it up)*
I'm blue	*(hold up blue card)*
I am yellow	*(hold up yellow card)*
Sometimes I'm blue	*(hold up blue card)*
Sometimes I'm yellow	*(hold up yellow card)*
Guess what I am now!	*(hold up both cards)*

• Reinforce the concepts of "tall" and "small" by pointing out things in the classroom. Is the door to the room tall or small? What about the windows?

Ask each child to name one thing in the room that is tall and one thing that is small.

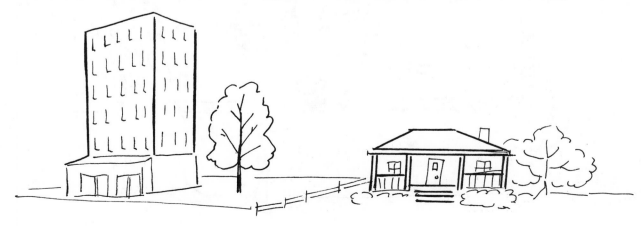

HERE'S OUR LITTLE PINE TREE

(Sung to the tune of "I'm a Little Teapot")

Traditional Melody

Here's our lit - tle pine tree, tall and straight.
Hang on all the tin - sel, shi - ny and bright.

Let's find the things so we can de - co - rate.
Put on the canes and we deck them just right.

First we want to put a star on top, then we
Fin - ally put some pre - sents for you and for me, then and

must be care - ful the balls don't pop.
we'll be read - y with our Christ - mas tree!

ACTIVITY

Teach the song using the following words.

Here's our little pine tree tall and straight.
Let's find the things so we can decorate.
First we want to put a star on top!
Then we must be careful the balls don't pop.

Hang on all the tinsel, shiny and bright.
Put on the canes and hook them just right.
Finally, put some presents for you and for me,
And we'll be ready with our Christmas tree.

Sing the song while decorating the classroom tree. Point out to the children the various items in the song, such as *star, tinsel, balls,* etc.

Let a child be the "tree." Make ornaments out of construction paper and have the rest of the class decorate the "tree." Or, draw a tree on a large piece of posterboard and secure it to the wall. Let the class tape ornaments on the tree—you can even make a game out of it, a sort of "Pin the Tail on the Donkey," using ornaments instead of tails. Call it "Put the Ornament on the Christmas Tree."

ADDITIONAL ACTIVITIES

• Talk about where Christmas trees come from. Read *The Little Fir Tree* to the class.

• Discuss with the children what an "evergreen" tree is and why it is still green in the wintertime, while other trees lose their leaves.

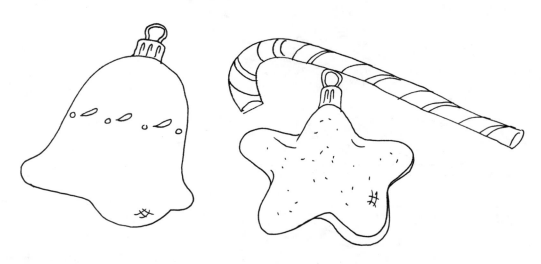

NINE LITTLE REINDEER

Words and Music by
"Miss Jackie" Weissman

Peek - ing thru the win - dow what do I see,
Skip - ping thru the sky with a click - e - ty click,

one lit - tle two lit - tle three lit - tle rein - deer.
four lit - tle five lit - tle six lit - tle rein - deer.

Bet - ter go to bed. Bet - ter close my eyes. If I want a

big sur - prise. Lis - ten to the roof top, what do I hear?

Seven lit - tle eight lit - tle nine lit - tle rein - deer rein - deer.

© 1980 Jackie Weissman
Recorded on *Sniggles, Squirrels and Chicken Pox, Vol. I*
Miss Jackie Music Co.

SKILLS: *Listening; rhythm; movement.*

ACTIVITY

Why is this song called "Nine Little Reindeer"?

Read the portion from the poem *A Visit from St. Nicholas* where the reindeer names are listed. Have the children count the names. Oops—only eight names! (Someone will soon discover that Rudolph is missing.)

Sing the song and act out the parts. Cup your hands in front of your eyes and "peek." Raise a finger for each number as you count the reindeer. Cup your hand behind your ear to "listen." Have the children skip around the room on "skipping through the sky."

ADDITIONAL ACTIVITIES

• The pentatonic melody of this song is gentle, soft and flowing. It lends itself to bell-like sounds. Triangles, bells, glockenspiels—any jingly instrument can be played with this song. Give each child an instrument and have them play on the numbers.

• In addition to the numbers, the key words in "Nine Little Reindeer" are "peeking," "listen" and "hear." Talk about things the children would like to peek through, listen to or hear.

• **Classification**— Pictures of animals with and without antlers can help the children learn to classify. A trip to the zoo to see the reindeer would be fun!

• **Movement**— Have the children pretend to be reindeer. How do reindeer walk? hop? jump? prance? run? Let them pretend they're pulling Santa's sleigh.

• **Math readiness**— Paste pictures of reindeer on cards and number the cards. Make two sets. The children pick a card from one set and match it with the same card from the other set.

• **Game**— Form a circle with nine children. They are the reindeer. One by one, each reindeer comes to the center of the circle and, using a reindeer name, says, "My name is _____ , and here is my trick." Then the child does a reindeer trick. (Make sure each child in the class gets a turn.)

MY DREYDEL

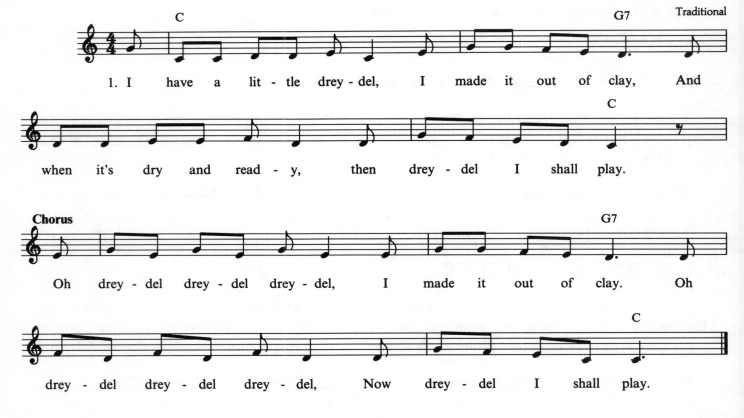

Traditional

1. I have a lit-tle drey-del, I made it out of clay, And when it's dry and read-y, then drey-del I shall play.

Chorus

Oh drey-del drey-del drey-del, I made it out of clay. Oh drey-del drey-del drey-del, Now drey-del I shall play.

2. My dreydel's always playful,
It loves to dance and spin.
A happy game of dreydel
Come play, now let's begin.
Oh, dreydel, dreydel, dreydel,
It loves to dance and spin.
Oh, dreydel, dreydel, dreydel,
Come play, now let's begin.

SKILL: *Learning about a Jewish holiday tradition.*

ACTIVITY

Have the children sit in a circle on the floor. Pick one child to be the first "dreydel." While the class sings the verse, the "dreydel" walks around the outside of the circle.

The "dreydel" steps into the middle of the circle for the chorus and, with eyes closed, hand outstretched and finger pointing, spins around. At the end of the song, whoever the "dreydel" is pointing to becomes the next "dreydel."

The class could clap while singing. (Note: be sure each child gets a turn at being the toy.)

ADDITIONAL ACTIVITY

• Make a dreydel for the class to play with. *(See illustration.)* Let each child have a turn at spinning the dreydel.

DREYDEL PATTERN

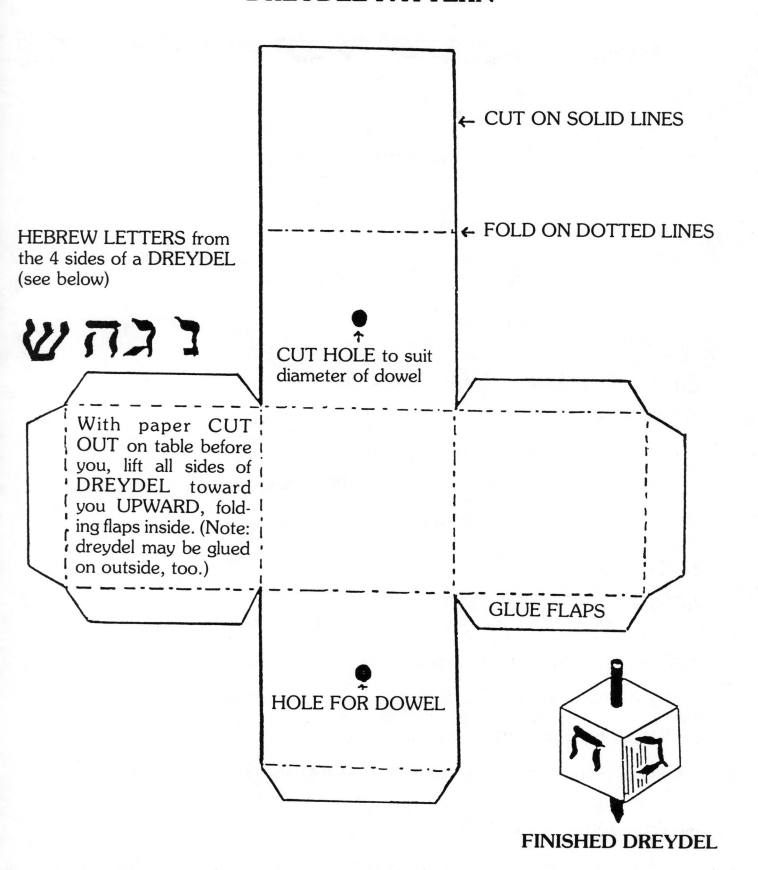

← CUT ON SOLID LINES

← FOLD ON DOTTED LINES

HEBREW LETTERS from the 4 sides of a DREYDEL (see below)

נגהש

CUT HOLE to suit diameter of dowel

With paper CUT OUT on table before you, lift all sides of DREYDEL toward you UPWARD, folding flaps inside. (Note: dreydel may be glued on outside, too.)

GLUE FLAPS

HOLE FOR DOWEL

FINISHED DREYDEL

WE WISH YOU A MERRY CHRISTMAS

Brightly

We wish you a mer - ry Christ - mas, We

wish you a mer - ry Christ - mas, We

wish you a mer - ry Christ - mas, And a hap - py New Year!

SKILL: *Learning to sign a holiday greeting.*

ACTIVITY

Here is a fun activity to teach children.

WE—Hold up three fingers to look like a "W"; move from right to left shoulder.

WISH—Form hand into a ball and place against chest.

YOU A—Point right index finger.

MERRY—Hit chest twice in upward strokes.

CHRISTMAS—Make the letter "C" with your hand and twist twice.

AND A—Pull hand across chest left to right.

HAPPY—Same as the word "merry."

NEW—Right hand in left palm; pull through.

YEAR—Make hands into fists; put fists together and circle around.

JACK IN THE BOX

Source Unknown

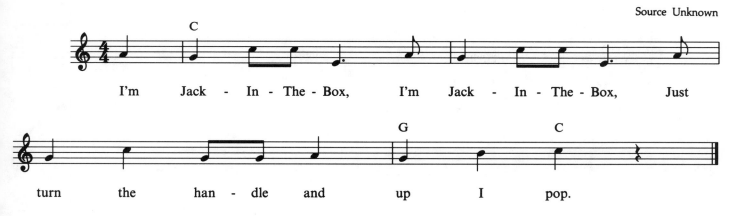

I'm   Jack - In - The - Box,   I'm   Jack - In - The - Box,   Just

turn   the   han - dle   and   up   I   pop.

SKILLS: *Listening; following directions; creative dramatics; gross motor skills.*

ACTIVITY

Bring a jack-in-the-box for the class to see and play with before teaching the song.

Have the children squat in a circle on the floor to pantomime the song. The teacher (or a selected child) turns the "handle" of each "jack-in-the-box" by shaking each child's arm. On the words "Up I pop!" everyone "pops up."

ADDITIONAL ACTIVITIES

• Make a game of the song. Have the children squat in a circle on the floor. One child is designated "It." While the class sings the song, "It" goes around the circle shaking each child's arm. The last one to be shook before everyone "pops up" becomes "It." (Make sure each child has a turn at being "It.")

• Talk about how toys work. Bring several toys to class that have some kind of mechanical feature. Show the class how each one works.

Ask the children which parts move. What happens when a button is pressed or some other part is moved? (Note: be sure to use toys that are non-toxic and have no sharp edges.)

OKKI-TOKKI-UNGA

Eskimo Song

SKILLS: *Sequencing a story; creative movement; language.*

ACTIVITY

This song and the motions that go with it illustrate a whale search, Eskimo style. Sing the song with the following motions.

Okki-tokki-unga, okki-tokki unga	*(make paddling motions,*
Hey Missa Day, Missa Doh, Missa Day	*as if paddling a canoe)*
Okki-tokki-unga, okki-tokki unga	*(make paddling motions,*
Hey Missa Day, Missa Doh, Missa Day	*as if paddling a canoe)*
Hexa-cola-misha-won-i	*(shade eyes and pretend*
Hexa-cola-misha-won-i	*to be scanning the sea)*

The teacher "narrates" the story while the children sing the song and do the above motions.

Teacher:

We are going to look for whales like the Eskimos do. First, we have to put on our boots. *(Everyone pretends to pull on boots.)* Next, we have to zip up our coats. *(Everyone pretends to zip up coats.)* Now, let's put our nets and ropes in the canoe. *(Pretend to put nets and ropes in canoe.)* Okay, get in the canoe. *(Pretend to get into canoe.)* Let's go!

Everyone:
Okki-tokki-unga, okki-tokki-unga,
Hey Missa Day, Missa Doh, Missa Day.
(Pretend to paddle canoe)

Teacher:
Let's look to see if we can find a whale.

Everyone:
Hexa-cola-misha-won-i,
Hexa-cola-misha-won-i.
(Pretend to scan horizon)

Teacher:
I don't see one, do you? Let's keep going.

Repeat the above exchange, then continue with the story.

Teacher:
Look! There's a whale! Let's paddle over to it! *(Sing chorus and paddle very quickly.)* Let's throw our nets out and try to catch it. *(Pretend to throw nets over whale.)* Now, tie the rope around its tail. *(Pretend to tie rope.)* Now, drag it into the canoe. *(Pretend to drag a very heavy whale into canoe.)* Let's take it to Seaworld! *(Sing chorus and paddle very slowly.)*

Teacher:
Can we find Seaworld from here? *(Sing verse, pretending to scan horizon; repeat and then go on.)* There's Seaworld! Let's paddle our canoe over to it! *(Sing chorus slowly—the canoe is still very heavy.)* Let's paddle in and let our whale go into the tank. *(Sing chorus and paddle a little faster.)*

Teacher:
Untie the rope. *(Pretend to untie the rope.)* Now, take off the net. *(Pretend to take the net off the whale.)* Now, let it go! *(Pretend to push the whale over the side of the canoe.)*

Teacher:
Now, let's go home!

Sing chorus one more time and paddle fast to get home.

ADDITIONAL ACTIVITIES

• Talk with the class about whales. Explain that they are the largest animals in the ocean. What other animals can they think of that live in the ocean?

• This song provides an excellent opportunity to talk about Eskimos and how their lifestyle differs from that of other Americans. Explain to the children that Eskimos live where it is very cold and there is lots of water. The canoe is their means of transportation and they have to dress very warmly.

• Make up more parts to the story, or change the story to a seal or walrus search instead of a whale search. The story is very open ended; you can add as much as you want!

OH, YOU PUSH THE DAMPER IN

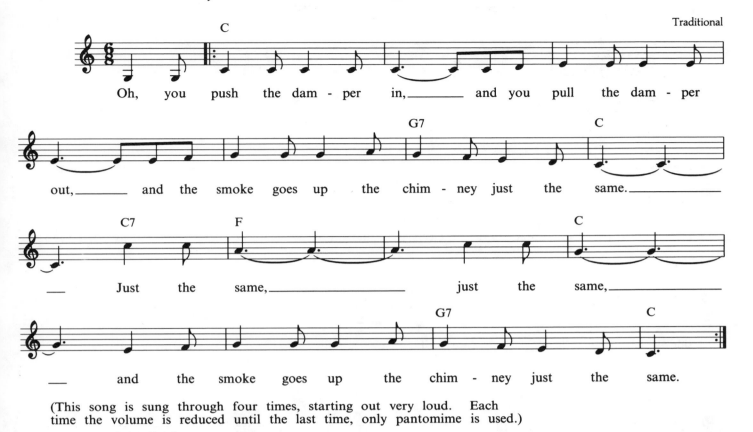

(This song is sung through four times, starting out very loud. Each time the volume is reduced until the last time, only pantomime is used.)

SKILLS: *Listening; verbalization.*

ACTIVITY

Explain to the children that a "damper" is a kind of plate that moves in and out to control the air flow in a chimney.

Sing the song while doing the following actions.

Oh, you push the damper in   *(pretend to push in damper)*
And you pull the damper out   *(pretend to pull out damper)*
And the smoke goes up the chimney   *(make a winding motion in the*
    just the same   *air with your hand)*
Just the same, just the same   *(shrug shoulders)*
And the smoke goes up the chimney   *(make a winding motion in the*
    just the same   *air with your hand)*

ADDITIONAL ACTIVITY

• Sing the song four times, starting out very loud. Sing it more quietly each time. On the last time through, do not sing—just do the motions.

TEN LITTLE FINGERS

Unknown

1. Ten lit - tle fin - gers and ten lit - tle toes,
2. Two lit - tle legs___ and two lit - tle feet,

Two shi - ny eyes___ and one lit - tle nose. Two lit - tle ears on the
Two lit - tle hands that are clean and neat, Two lit - tle arms that go

sides of my head, One llit - tle tongue that is col - ored red.
up and down, One lit - tle face that can smile or frown.

Coda

Now I have coun - ted all of me; I hope you like the per - son you see.

Reprinted by permission of
DAVID C. COOK PUBLISHERS, INC.

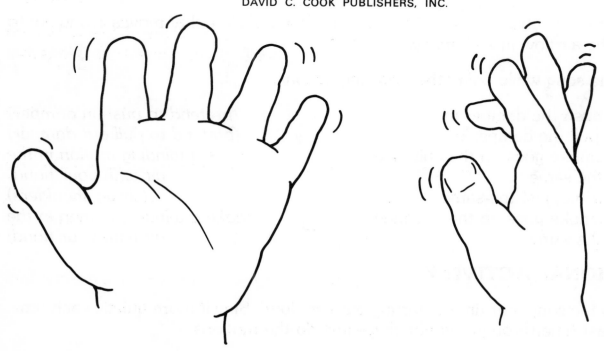

SKILLS: *Learning body parts; developing self-awareness.*

ACTIVITY

Sing the song with the following actions.

Ten little fingers *(hold up both hands, wiggle fingers)*
And ten little toes *(point to feet or wiggle toes)*
Two shiny eyes *(point to both eyes)*
And one little nose *(touch your nose)*
Two little ears on the sides of my head *(touch both ears)*
One little tongue that is colored red *(stick out tongue)*

Two little legs *(touch legs)*
And two little feet *(kick feet)*
Two little hands that are clean and neat *(hold up hands)*
Two little arms that go up and down *(make up-and-down motions with arms)*
One little face that can smile or frown *(smile, then frown)*

Now I have counted all of me
I hope you like the person you see

Note: language-delayed children can point to the body parts rather than sing the song.

ADDITIONAL ACTIVITIES

• The children sit in a circle. Give each child a turn at playing "three guesses."

Have one child stand in the middle of the circle. Whisper in the child's ear which body part you want him or her to describe. Then, have the child name three things that can be done with the body part.

Two little legs—You can run with them, you can jump with them, you can walk with them.

Ten little fingers—You can paint with them, you can eat French fries with them, you can tie a bow with them.

Let the rest of the class make three guesses as to what the body part is. Let each child have a chance to describe a body part.

• Make up other words to the song to describe other body parts. Ask the children for suggestions.

ABC (SOUP) SONG
(Sung to the tune of "Twinkle, Twinkle, Little Star")

Traditional

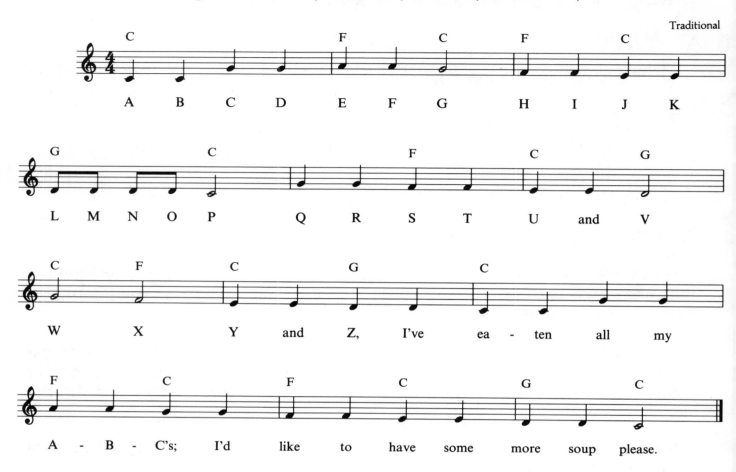

A B C D E F G H I J K

L M N O P Q R S T U and V

W X Y and Z, I've ea - ten all my

A - B - C's; I'd like to have some more soup please.

SKILL: *Recognizing letters of the alphabet.*

ACTIVITY

Make alphabet flash cards by writing the each letter on a 3″x5″ card with a bold magic marker. Decorate a large, round container to look like a soup can and put the letter cards in the can.

Let each child draw a letter from the can and tell you what letter they have drawn.

Variation: serve the children some alphabet soup for lunch (or a bowl of Alpha-Bits cereal). Ask each child to identify a letter in his or her bowl.

ADDITIONAL ACTIVITIES

• Sing the song through several times with the class. Give each child an alphabet flash card, then sing the song very slowly. Instruct the children to hold up the correct letter card when the letter is sung in the song.

To simpifly the activity, line the children up in order—the first child as "A," the second as "B," the third as "C," and so on. If you have more flash cards than children, give some of the children two cards—for example, the first would hold "A" and "B," the second "C" and "D," etc.

• Give each child a large cut-out letter with which their names begin. Let them color the letters with crayons.

Check color as well as letter recognition: go around the circle asking each child to name his or her letter and letter color.

THE SNOWMAN

Unknown

I made a lit-tle snow-man. I made him big and round. I

made him from a snow-ball I rolled u-pon the ground. He has two eyes, a nose, a mouth, a

love - ly scarf of red; He e - ven has some but-tons and a

hat u - pon his head. Melt, melt, melt, melt, melt, melt, melt, melt.

SKILLS: *Listening; story sequencing; science/weather concepts; language development; ascending scale.*

ACTIVITY

Let the children imagine they are snowmen—first growing tall, then slowly melting.

Talk about why the snowman melted. Did it melt slow or fast? What else melts?

Take an ice cube from the freezer and watch it melt. Does it take a long time? How long does it take a piece of ice to melt in your mouth? What does ice become when it melts? What does snow become when it melts?

ADDITIONAL ACTIVITIES

• Make a snowman out of white poster paper. Secure it to the wall. Make eyes, nose, mouth, scarf and hat out of construction paper and put tape on the backs of the pieces so the children can tape them onto the snowman.

As you sing the song with the class, let the children dress the snowman. Sing the song over and over until each child has had a chance to put an item on the snowman.

• On a snowy winter day, take the class outside and build a real snowman. Visit it each day and observe whether it has melted. Keep track of how many days it takes for the snowman to melt.

• Use the song to teach the class about "up" and "down" in music. Show them how to play the song on the piano or on Orff instruments—the song goes up the C scale first, then back down on the last line. Let the children have a turn at playing the song on an instrument.

TINY TIM

Traditional

1. I had a lit - tle bro - ther; his name was Ti - ny Tim. I put him in the bath - tub to see if he could swim.

2. He drank up all the water; He ate up all the soap;
   And now he's home sick in bed with bubbles in his throat

3. In came the Doctor; in came the Nurse;
   In came the Lady with the alligator purse.

4. "Measles," said the Doctor; "Mumps," said the Nurse;
   "Chicken pox," said the Lady with the alligator purse.

5. "Penicillin," said the Doctor; "Penicillin," said the Nurse
   "Penicillin," said the Lady with the alligator purse.

6. "I don't want the Doctor, I don't want the Nurse,
   I don't want the Lady with the alligator purse."

7. Out went the Doctor; out went the Nurse;
   Out went the Lady with the alligator purse.

SKILLS: *Socialization; dramatic play.*

ACTIVITY

Act out the song with the class.

Choose children to be these characters: "Tiny Tim," "Doctor," "Nurse," "Lady with alligator purse."

Use the following for props:

Large cardboard box (for the bathtub)
Purse for the "Lady" (put a picture of an alligator on it)
Jar of bubbles and wand (for "Tiny Tim" to blow when he "eats" the soap)
First-aid kit or small black bag (for the "Doctor")
Nurse's hat (can be made from paper)

ADDITIONAL ACTIVITY

• For a variation on the play, make puppets out of popsicle sticks to represent the characters in the song. Let each child have a turn at playing a part.

INKY-DINKY-DOO

Traditional

My hand on my self, what do I see,

This is my Think - box - er oh_____ Ma - ma dear.
Eye - wink - er
Nose - smel - ler

Think - box - er, Think - box - er, Ink - y - dink - y
(Eye - wink - er,)
(Nose - smel - ler,)

doo. That's what I learned in my school.

SKILLS: *Sequencing; fun.*

ACTIVITY

Ask the children to form a circle. Sing through the song a verse at a time, pointing out the particular body part in each verse.

Put my hand on my self, self,
What do I see, see?
This is my think-boxer, oh Mama dear.   *(put hand on head)*
Think-boxer, think-boxer, inky-dinky-doo.
That's what I learned in my school.

Put my hand on my self, self,
What do I see, see?
This is my eye-winker, oh Mama dear.   *(point to eye)*
Eye-winker,
Think-boxer,   *(put hand on head)*
Inky-dinky-doo.
That's what I learned in my school.

This is my nose-smeller, oh Mama dear.   *(point to nose)*
Nose-smeller,
Eye-winker,   *(point to eye)*
Think-boxer,   *(put hand on head)*
Inky-dinky-doo.
That's what I learned in my school.

Continue the song with these verses: ear-listener, mouth-souper, chest-protector, tummy-warmer, hip-wiggler, knee-bender, ankle-breaker, foot-warmer, kid-huggers (arms).

ADDITIONAL ACTIVITIES

• Line up 12 children (one for each verse) in front of the group. Assign each child a body part.

When the rest of the class sings the song, each child points out the body part when that verse is sung. (For example, the first child is assigned "think-boxer." When the class sings "This is my think-boxer," that child puts a hand on his/her head.)

• Variation: pass out pictures (cut from magazines) of body parts. Have each child hold up the appropriate picture when the verse is sung.

SIX LITTLE SNOWMEN

Source Unknown

1. Six lit - tle peo - ple all made of snow,

Six lit - tle snow - men stand - ing in a row,

Out came the sun and stayed all day,

One lit - tle snow - man mel - ted a - way.

Verse 2
Five little snowmen all made of snow
Five little snowmen standing in a row
Out came the sun and shined all day
One little snowman melted away
(Continue with four snowmen, etc.)

SKILLS: *Counting; creative dramatics.*

ACTIVITY

Sing through the song with the children, then add the following motions.

Six little people	*(hold up six fingers)*
All made of snow	*(pretend to roll a snowball)*
Six little snowmen	*(hold up six fingers)*
Standing in a row	*(point to imaginary snowmen on each word)*
Out came the sun	*(lift arms above head in a big circle)*
And stayed all day	*(keep arms circled overhead)*
One little snowman	*(hold up one finger)*
Melted away	*(make wavy motions with your hands all the way down to the floor)*

Repeat the motions with each verse, holding up the appropriate number of fingers for "five little snowmen," "four little snowmen," etc.

ADDITIONAL ACTIVITIES

• Act out the song.

Ask six children to be "snowmen" and one child to be the "sun." Line up the "snowmen" in a row. Instruct the "sun" to go to the line and touch one of the "snowmen" on the head. That "snowman" slowly sits down on the floor.

The "sun" repeats the action with each verse of the song until all "snowmen" are sitting on the floor. Choose a new cast of characters and act out the song again.

You might want to start with the same number in the song as you have children in the class. For example, if there are ten children, sing "Ten little snowmen." The class could all line up and be the "snowmen" and the teacher could be the "sun."

• On a snowy day, take the children outside and build six snowmen of their own. Watch the figures for a few days to see which one melts first. Do they melt one at a time or all at once? Do the ones in the sun melt faster than the ones in the shade?

CLAP YOUR HANDS

American Folk Song

With Spirit

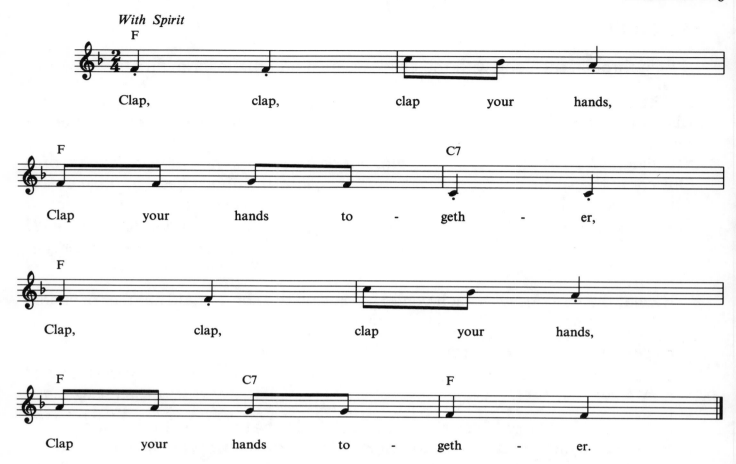

Clap, clap, clap your hands,

Clap your hands to - geth - er,

Clap, clap, clap your hands,

Clap your hands to - geth - er.

SKILLS: *Practicing following directions; experiencing isolated body movements.*

ACTIVITY

Ask the children to stand in a circle. Sing the song, doing the following motions to each verse.

Clap, clap, clap your hands   *(everyone claps hands)*

Stomp, stomp, stomp your feet   *(everyone stomps feet)*

Slap, slap, slap your thighs   *(everyone slaps thighs)*

Ideas for additional verses might include "swing your arms," "jump up high," "skip around the circle," "wave goodbye," "walk like ducks," "march around the circle," "move in slow motion."

Ask the children to think of other motions.

ADDITIONAL ACTIVITY

• Circle the children and give each one a rhythm instrument. Change the words of the song to go with the instruments. Go around the circle and sing a verse for each kind of instrument. Have the children with the instruments named in the song play their instruments while the rest of the class sings.

Tap, tap, tap the drum   *(all children with drums tap them)*

Shake, shake, shake the tambourine   *(all children with tambourines shake them)*

Ring, ring, ring the bells   *(all children with sleighbells or triangle bells ring them)*

Trade instruments so everyone gets a chance to play something different.

GROUNDHOG

Words and Music by
"Miss Jackie" Weissman

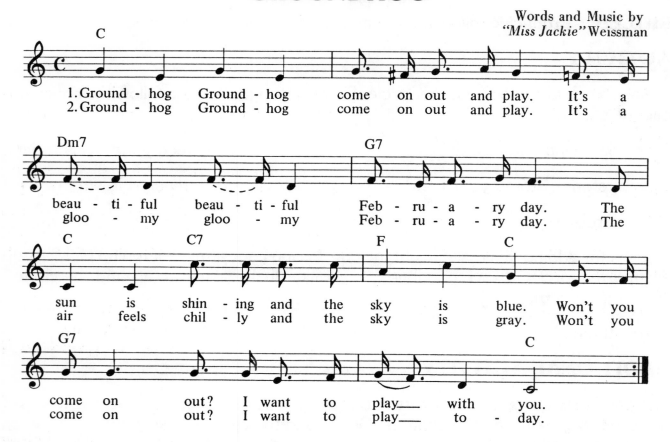

1. Ground - hog   Ground - hog   come   on   out   and   play.   It's   a
2. Ground - hog   Ground - hog   come   on   out   and   play.   It's   a

beau - ti - ful   beau - ti - ful   Feb - ru - a - ry   day.   The
gloo - my   gloo - my   Feb - ru - a - ry   day.   The

sun   is   shin - ing   and   the   sky   is   blue.   Won't   you
air   feels   chil - ly   and   the   sky   is   gray.   Won't   you

come   on   out?   I   want   to   play___   with   you.
come   on   out?   I   want   to   play___   to - day.

© 1980 Jackie Weissman
Recorded on *Sniggles, Squirrels and Chicken Pox, Vol. II*
Miss Jackie Music Co.

SKILL: *Learning about "Groundhog Day."*

ACTIVITY

Have the children sit on the floor in a circle. Tell them the groundhog story: it is commonly believed that if the groundhog sees its shadow when it comes out of hibernation on February 2, there will be six more weeks of winter.

The Groundhog Game—Make several suns and clouds out of construction paper, one of each for each child in the class *(see patterns on page 185).* Have the children sit in a circle on the floor. Designate one child to be the "groundhog," who sits in the middle of the circle with eyes closed. The other children watch the teacher for directions: if the teacher holds up a sun, the children hold up their suns; if the teacher holds up a cloud, the children hold up their clouds.

Tell the "groundhog" to open his eyes. If he sees clouds, then he chooses a "shadow" from the children in the circle; the "shadow" then becomes the "groundhog." If the "groundhog" sees suns, then he stays in the middle of the circle (the "groundhog's hole"). (Make sure each child has a turn at being the "groundhog.")

ADDITIONAL ACTIVITY

● Talk about hibernation. Explain it to the children: how some animals, such as groundhogs and bears, "sleep" during the winter months.

What do other animals do during the winter? For instance, birds fly south to warmer places. Ask the children what their pets do during the winter. What do people do during the winter?

A PEANUT SAT ON A RAILROAD TRACK

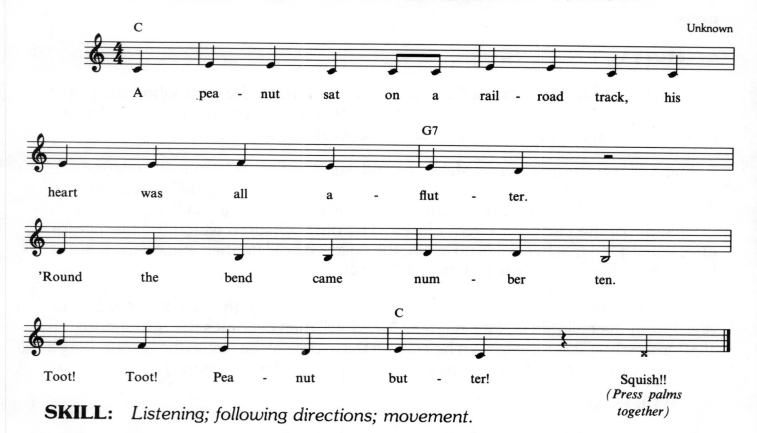

Unknown

A pea - nut sat on a rail - road track, his heart was all a - flut - ter. 'Round the bend came num - ber ten. Toot! Toot! Pea - nut but - ter! Squish!! *(Press palms together)*

SKILL: *Listening; following directions; movement.*

ACTIVITY

Sing this song with the following motions.

A peanut sat on a railroad track
Sit cross-legged in a circle and make a fist with one hand; rest it on your thigh

His heart was all a-flutter
Cross hands over heart and beat chest

'Round the bend came Number Ten
Make a large circle in the air with one hand, then hold up ten fingers

Toot! Toot! Peanut butter!
Pull imaginary cord twice on "Toot! Toot!" Clap and rub hands together on "Squish!"

ADDITIONAL ACTIVITIES

• Make homemade peanut butter!

Shell peanuts. Put one cup of peanuts, with a teaspoon of vegetable or corn oil, into a blender. Blend until smooth and spread on crackers, bread or celery.

• Make small puppets by drawing faces on the peanut shells.

I-TISKET, I-TASKET

Traditional

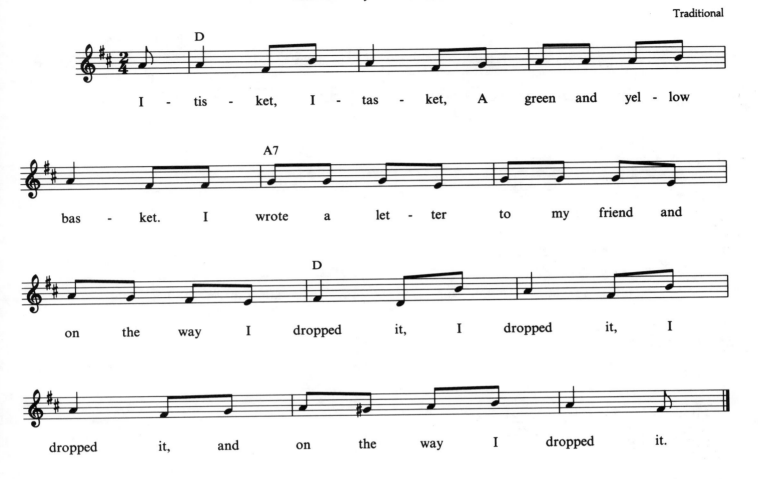

SKILL: *Learning to read someone's name.*

ACTIVITY

Decorate a basket with red and white ribbons. Fill it with paper hearts on which the children's names have been written.

Choose one person to start the game. As the first part of the song is sung, the child chooses a heart from the basket. On the words "on the way I dropped it," stop the song briefly and ask the child if they know the name on the heart. (If he/she doesn't recognize it, tell it to him/her.)

Sing the last part of the song while the child delivers the heart. The game continues as each child has a heart delivered and becomes the new "deliverer."

ADDITIONAL ACTIVITIES

● Use this song for other holidays—May Day, Easter, etc.

● Use letters to deliver; the "deliverer" identifies the letter or numbers or colors.

HOORAY FOR MISTER LINCOLN

Words and Music by
"Miss Jackie" Weissman

Hoo - ray for Mis - ter Lin - coln. Hoo - ray for Mis - ter Wash - ing - ton.

They helped to make our coun - try great. _____ Hoo -

ray for Mis - ter Lin - coln. Hoo - ray for Mis - ter Wash - ing - ton.

Now is the time to cel - e - brate. _____ I'm

proud to be an A - mer - i - can, proud of the red white and

blue, oo. _____ Hoo - ray for Mis - ter Lin - coln. Hoo -

ray for Mis - ter Wash - ing - ton. Hap - py birth - day,

hap - py birth - day, hap - py birth - day to you. _____

Recorded on *Sniggles, Squirrels and Chicken Pox, Vol. I*
Miss Jackie Music Co.

SKILL: *Learning about our country's history.*

ACTIVITY

This song leads to much discussion and has many important vocabulary words: "Lincoln," "Washington," "celebrate," "country," "American," "red," "white," "blue."

Have the children make their own American flags. Let them wave their flags while marching around the room singing the song.

ADDITIONAL ACTIVITIES

• Study the American flag. Count the stars. Why are there 50? Look at the flags of other countries. Are they similar to our flag? Do they have the same colors? What do the colors mean?

• Say (or shout) "Hip hip, hooray!" two times. On the third time say only "Hip hip," and on the word "hooray" start singing the song.

• Each time you sing the word "hooray," lead the children in a different action— stamping feet, clapping hands, and so on.

• March with your feet. March with your hands (fingers together, palms in). March with your fingers.

• Have a "Red, White and Blue Day." Wear those colors. Use only red, white and blue crayons or paints for the day. Have red, white and blue treats.

HOW WOULD YOU SAY HELLO?

Traditional

SKILLS: *Learning to say "hello," "goodbye" and "thank you" in other languages; learning about people in other countries.*

ACTIVITY

Have the children sit in a circle. Teach them the song a line at a time. Once they've learned the song, use it as a greeting or to introduce a lesson about another culture.

TEACHER: If you were a little Spanish boy, how would you say "hello"?
BOYS: If I were a little Spanish boy, I'd say, "buenos dias."

TEACHER: If you were a little Spanish girl, how would you say "goodbye"?
GIRLS: If I were a little Spanish girl, I'd say, "adios."

TEACHER: If you were little Spanish children, how would you say "thank you"?
CHILDREN: If we were little Spanish children, we'd say, "muchas gracias."

Try the song with other languages—French: *bonjour* ("hello"), *au revoir* ("goodbye"), *merci* ("thank you"); German: *gutentag* ("hello"), *auf wiedersen* ("goodbye"), *danke schoen* ("thank you").

ADDITIONAL ACTIVITIES

• Bring a globe to class to show the children where Spanish-speaking countries are. (Also show them where France and Germany are, if you've taught them the song using those languages.)

Design a lesson plan on one country each month. Find pictures in encyclopedias or use travel posters to show the children what the particular country looks like.

• If you have children from other countries in your class, this song is a wonderful opportunity for them to share their culture with the others. For instance, ask a Japanese or Indian child to bring clothing or other items from home to show the class. Ask the child how to say "hello," "goodbye" and "thank you" in his or her language. Incorporate the new language into the song.

India

Japan

TURN, CINNAMON, TURN

American Singing Game

With a swing

All up and down my hon-ey, All up and down we go. That la-dy's a-rock-in' her su-gar lump, That la-dy's a rock-in' her su-gar lump, That la-dy's a rock-in' her su-gar lump, Oh turn, cin-na-mon, turn.

SKILLS: *Encouraging social interaction; gross motor skills.*

ACTIVITY

Ask the children to stand in a circle. Do the following dance while singing the song.

All up and down, my honey,
All up and down we go.
Teacher begins dance by walking around the group and clapping while singing.

That lady's a rockin' her sugar lump,
That lady's a rockin' her sugar lump.
Teacher chooses a partner to be the "sugar lump."

That lady's a rockin' her sugar lump.
Partners face each other, hold hands, and swing arms back and forth.

Oh, turn, Cinnamon, turn.
Partners continue to hold hands and walk around in a circle.

Sing the song again, but this time the "sugar lump" chooses a new partner and repeats the dance. The teacher also chooses a new partner and repeats the dance.

Repeat the song until all children are dancing.

ADDITIONAL ACTIVITY

- Sing the song doing the following actions while standing in place.

All up and down, my honey,
Move arms up and down, then hug yourself.

All up and down we go.
Move arms up and down.

That lady's a rockin' her sugar lump,
That lady's a rockin' her sugar lump.
That lady's a rockin' her sugar lump.
Make a fist and place it in the palm of your other hand; rock it back and forth.

Oh, turn, Cinnamon, turn.
Turn around in place.

WILL YOU BE MY VALENTINE?

Words and music by
JERRY MALONEY

Will you be my val - en - tine, my val - en - tine, my val - en - tine?

Will you be my val - en - tine, my ver - y spec - ial friend?

_____ is my val - en - tine, my val - en - tine, my val - en - tine.

Child's name

_____ is my val - en - tine, my ver - y spec - ial friend.

Child's name

SKILLS: *Encouraging friendship and social skills.*

ACTIVITY

Have the children prepare a Valentine's Day card for their "Valentine" in class. Pair off the children so everyone has a Valentine. (If there is one child left over, that child can be the teacher's Valentine.)

Have the class sing the song as they exchange Valentine's Day cards.

ADDITIONAL ACTIVITIES

- Add other verses to the song, such as:

Do you have a Valentine?
Yes, I have a Valentine.

Who is your Valentine?
_____ is my Valentine.

Valentines are fun to give.
Valentines are fun to get.

- Have the children prepare Valentine's Day cards for their favorite people—parents, sisters, brothers, other relatives, teachers, school bus drivers, etc. Or, make one huge Valentine's Day card for another class (or from your class to itself).

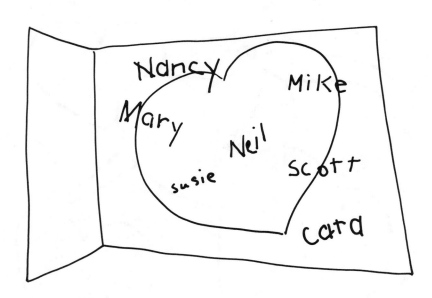

ONE RED VALENTINE

Source Unknown

One red val - en - tine, Two red val - en - tines,

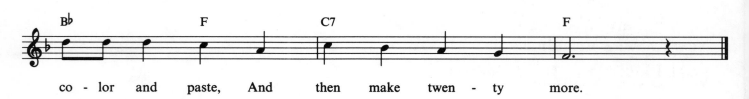

Three red val - en - tines four, I'll snip and cut and

co - lor and paste, And then make twen - ty more.

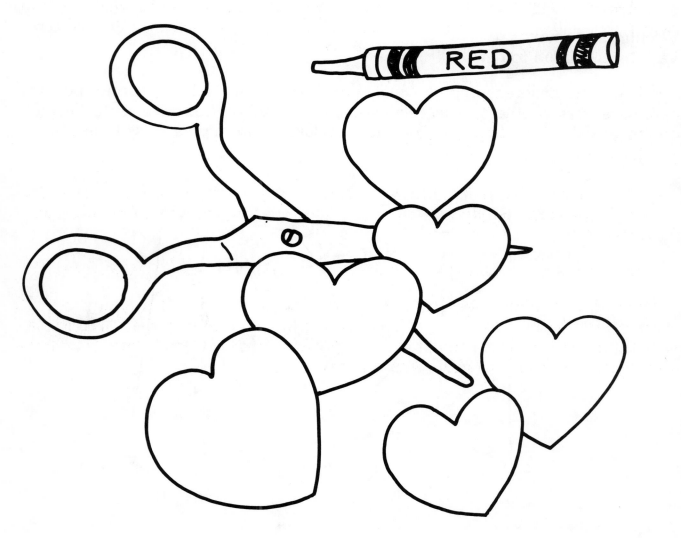

SKILLS: *Counting; color recognition; making Valentines for the class.*

ACTIVITY

Make several hearts out of flannel or red construction paper backed with flannel *(see pattern on page 185).* As the class sings the song, let one child put the first "red Valentine" on the flannel board, another put the second one on the flannel board, etc., until all Valentines are on the board.

You may want to add verses to accommodate more than four hearts. For example:

Five red Valentines, six red Valentines,
Seven red Valentines, eight.
I'll snip and cut and color and paste
And make them all look great.

ADDITIONAL ACTIVITIES

• Make the hearts out of different colors of construction paper and make up verses to match the colors. Hold up a heart and have the class sing the song, substituting the color of heart you are holding for the word "red."

One blue Valentine, two blue Valentines,
Three blue Valentines, four. . . .

One purple Valentine, two purple Valentines,
Three purple Valentines, four. . . .

• Help the children make Valentines for the class party (or to take home). Give each child a heart shape cut from white construction paper and let them use crayons to decorate their Valentines.

You could use the children's Valentines as you sing the song with color words.

• Go on a "Valentine hunt." Hide the Valentines the children made around the room. (Note: "hide" them so they are easy to find!) As the children find Valentines, have them bring them to you. Paste them onto a large piece of poster board to make a Valentine's Day collage to display in the classroom.

I LOVE YOU

By JANET REZNICEK

I love you, I love you, yes I do!

Used with permission

SKILLS: *Self-concept; learning others' names; language skills; using sign language.*

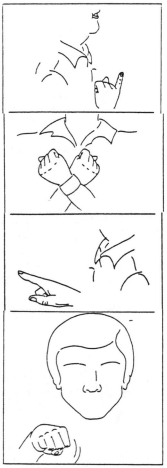

I

The "I" hand is placed at the chest.
Origin: Using the initial letter while indicating self
Usage: I will go with you

Love, Dear

The "S" hands are crossed at the wrist and pressed to the heart. (Or use the open hands.)
Origin: Pressing to one's heart
Usage: My first **love**
　　　　Our **dear** friend

You

Point the index finger out. (For the plural "you," point the index finger out and move from left to right.)
Origin: Natural sign
Usage: **You** have one vote
　　　　All of **you** are improving

Yes

Shake the right "S" up and down in front of you. (Agreement is also indicated by shaking the right "Y" up and down.)
Origin: The fist, representing the head, nods in agreement
Usage: **Yes,** I will go

ACTIVITY

Ask the class, "Who wants to be loved?" Pick a child and say, "*(Child's name)* does!" Sing the song to the child, then have the class sing it.

Sing the song to each child in the class. (For a more personal touch, hug the child after singing the song.)

ADDITIONAL ACTIVITIES

• Use this song as a greeting song for Valentine's day. Sing to each child as he or she enters the room.

• Sign the song for the class and teach them to sign it as well.

WE ARE FINE MUSICIANS

SKILL: *Learning "far" and "near" concepts.*

ACTIVITY

Discuss far and near. Do objects change in size when they are far away? Why do they look larger when near, smaller when far? Ask some children to stand far and near to the rest of the group.

Line up your musicians at the opposite side of the room and let them come from far away while singing the song.

Pass out instruments to the children and ask them to play as they sing. Would they like to parade as they play their music?

Talk about the different sounds we can make with our bodies: clapping hands, snapping fingers, tapping toes, slapping thighs. Practice making body sounds while singing.

ADDITIONAL ACTIVITY

• Change this into a movement activity instead of playing instruments by replacing "We sing" with "We slide/skip/walk/turn/etc."

SPRING IS COMING

Unknown

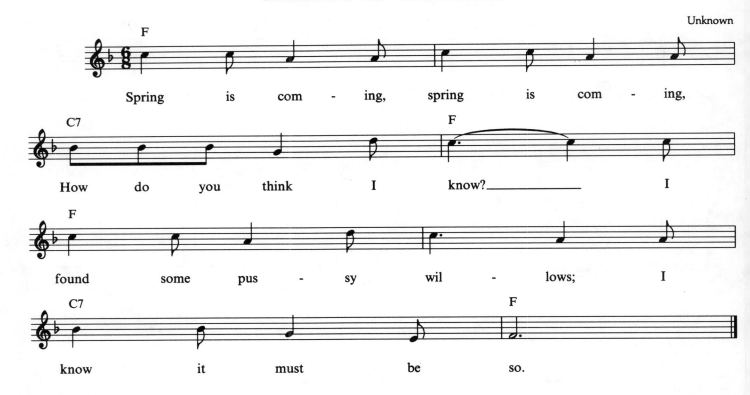

Spring is com - ing, spring is com - ing,

How do you think I know?_____ I

found some pus - sy wil - lows; I

know it must be so.

SKILLS: *Learning about seasons; listening skills; language development.*

ACTIVITY

Sing this song with the children. Ask them to name other signs of spring that they've noticed: green grass, flowers, robins, etc.

Display several signs of spring on a flannel board—a robin, flower, tree, pussy willow *(see patterns on pages 186 through 188)*—along with pictures of winter (a snowflake, snowman, bare tree).

ADDITIONAL ACTIVITIES

• Change the words to represent a different season. For example:

Fall is coming, fall is coming.
How do you think I know?
I saw a little pumpkin;
I know it must be so.

Use the flannel board to display pictures of fall. Include pictures of spring and summer and ask the children to remove all pictures that are not about fall.

• Take a walk outside on a nice day. Do this with the class during each season of the year.

Take along a notebook and jot down everything the children notice. For instance, in the fall they may see lots of red and orange leaves. Ask them what they see as they walk. How does the air feel? Is it hot or cool?

On the next seasonal walk, remind them of what they saw and heard. How are things different now? How are the trees different? What's different about the grass? Do they see something now that wasn't there on the last walk?

THE LEPRECHAUN SONG

Words: *Miss Jackie* Weissman
Jerry Maloney
Music: *Miss Jackie* Weissman

1., 5. Out in the deep dark for - est,
2. Pat - rick Le - pre - chaun stood up
3. Pat - rick's shoes are stur - dy, strong

Un - der a tree so green Two lit - tle le - pre-chauns
And said, "My shoes are grand." "Oh Blar-ney," Mike said
And per - fect for a king. Mich - ael's shoes are

mak - ing shoes for the fair - y king and queen.
"My shoes are the fin - est in this land."
shi - ny bright and per - fect for the

queen. 4. The king and queen ar - rived just then and

saw their shoes of green. "B' - gor - rah and B' -

gosh," they said, "They're the fin - est I've ev - er seen."

©1985 Jackie Weissman

SKILL: *Learning about an Irish myth.*

ACTIVITY

Leprechauns are mythical people who live in the forests of Ireland. They are wrinkled little old men who are very cranky. They live alone, far from the towns, and their main occupation is making shoes and boots for the *shees* (fairies) of Ireland. People often try to catch—or even just see—a leprechaun, but so far no one has been successful.

This song is meant just for fun, while exposing the children to the folklore of other countries. There are some fun words to learn—"blarney," "begorrah," "b'gosh"—and this is a good time to explain to the children that all countries have their myths: goblins, ghosts, leprechauns, tooth fairies and the like.

You can also talk about "Snow White and the Seven Dwarfs" and other fairy tales. Explain that in olden days, before television, people would tell each other these stories for entertainment. People were superstitious then, and nobody was really sure if these mythical creatures existed or not.

This song is a creative dramatic song. The words lend themselves to being acted out. Act out Patrick's and Michael's cobbling. How can they mime pride in their finished work?

IF YOU WERE A FARMER
(Did You Ever See a Lassie?)

Traditional Melody

1. Oh, _____ if you were a farm - er, a
2. I would gath - er eggs for break - fast, for

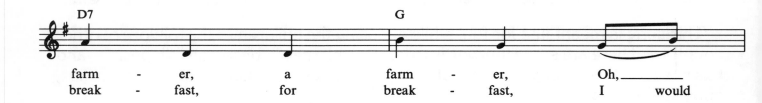

farm - er, a farm - er, Oh, _____
break - fast, for break - fast, I would

if you were a farm - er,
gath - er eggs for break - fast,

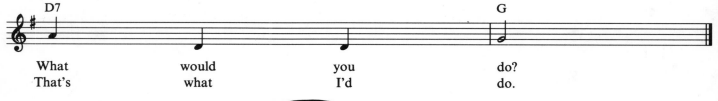

What would you do?
That's what I'd do.

SKILLS: *Learning about occupations; creative dramatics.*

ACTIVITY

Do the following actions while singing the verses.

Oh, if you were a farmer, a farmer, a farmer,
Oh, if you were a farmer, what would you do?

I would gather eggs for breakfast,   *(pretend to put eggs into a basket)*
For breakfast, for breakfast.
I would gather eggs for breakfast,
That's what I'd do.

I would ride the horse to pasture . . .   *(pretend to ride horse)*

I would milk the cow each morning . . .   *(sit on the floor and make
milking motions with hands over a pail*

I would feed the baby chickens . . .   *(throw seed on ground from a pail)*

I'd go plowing on a tractor . . .   *(steer the tractor up and down
the field; pretend to "drive")*

ADDITIONAL ACTIVITY

- Change the words to sing about other occupations. For example:

If you were a doctor. . . what would you do?
I would listen to a heartbeat . . .
I would ask you to say "aah". . .

If you were an astronaut . . . what would you do?
I would walk upon the moon . . .
I would ride in a big rocket . . .

If you were a firefighter. . . what would you do?
I would ride in a fire engine . . .
I would put out all the fires . . .

Ask the children for more ideas. Make up your own verses and actions to go with them.

OH CHESTER

Traditional

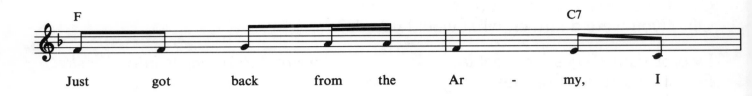

Oh   Ches - ter   have   you   heard   a - bout   Har - ry,

Just   got   back   from   the   Ar - my,   I

hear   he   knows   how   to   wear   his   clothes,   hip -

hip   hoo - ray   for   the   Ar - my.

SKILL: *Developing coordination and listening; lots of fun!*

ACTIVITY

Do the following actions while singing the song.

Oh Chester	*Hands on chest*
Have you heard	*Hands on ears*
About Harry?	*Hands on hair*
Just got back	*Hands on chest, then on back*
From the army	*Point to arm, then to yourself*
I	*Point to eye*
Hear	*Point to ear*
He knows	*Point to nose*
How to wear his clothes	*Touch clothes*
Hip hip hooray	*Hands pat hips*
For the army!	*Point to arm, then to yourself.*

Sing the song slowly at first. Each time you repeat the song, go faster and faster.

ADDITIONAL ACTIVITY

- Practice singing both softly and loudly.

Sing the song without the actions. Have the class sing loudly on the first few lines: "Oh Chester, have you heard about Harry? Just got back from the Army." Then, sing softly on the last few lines: "I hear he knows how to wear his clothes. Hip, hip, hooray for the army!"

Switch—sing softly on the first part and loudly on the last part.

Try dividing the class into two groups. Have one group sing the loud part and the other sing the soft part.

TWO LITTLE BLACKBIRDS

Two lit - tle black - birds sit - ting on a hill;

One named Jack and the oth - er named Jill;

Fly a - way, Jack! Fly a - way, Jill!

Come back, Jack, Come back, Jill.

SKILLS: *Increasing vocabulary; encouraging creativity.*

ACTIVITY

You and the children will have fun when putting the following motions to this song.

Two little blackbirds sitting on a hill
Hold up pointer finger of each hand

One named Jack and one named Jill
Wiggle "Jack" and then wiggle "Jill"

Fly away, Jack
Wiggle finger behind back in a flying motion

Fly away, Jill
Wiggle other finger behind back in a flying motion

Come back, Jack
Bring "Jack" flying back

Come back, Jill
Bring Jill back

ADDITIONAL ACTIVITIES

• Here is a song that can be new every time that you sing it. Ask the children to help you make up verses about what you're learning.

If you're learning colors, change the verse to "blue birds" or "orange birds," etc. At Halloween, sing about "ghosties that fly away," "pumpkins that roll away" and "black cats that sneak away."

For learning about animals, change the words to such as these:

Little turtles—waddle away
Angry alligators—slither away
Fluffy bunnies—hop away

• Use the song to teach about animals, as in the above example. Sing the song about an animal, then have the children act like the animal they've just sung about.

• Make birds of different colors to put on a flannel board. Let each child pick a bird and put it on the flannel board. Have the class sing about the color that the child puts on the board.

SIX BIG COWS

Unknown

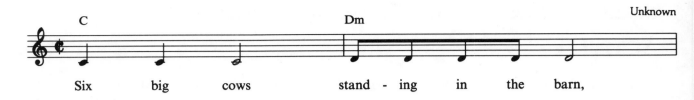

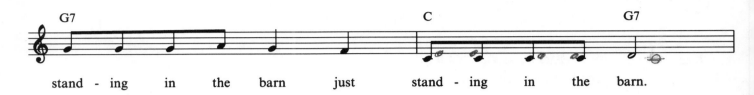

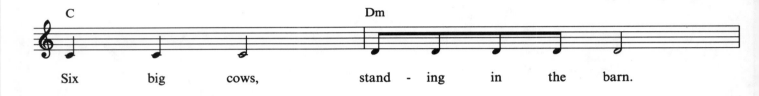

SKILLS: *Listening and verbal skills; learning about animals and animal sounds; counting.*

ACTIVITY

Here is a fingerplay for this song.

Six big cows   *(hold up six fingers)*
Standing in the barn   *(hold pointer and middle*
Standing in the barn   *fingers in upside-down "V")*
Just standing in the barn.
Six big cows   *(hold up six fingers)*
Standing in the barn   *(upside-down "V" with*
Moo, moo, moo.   *pointer and middle fingers)*

Five little pigs   *(hold up five fingers)*
Rolling in the mud   *(make two fists and roll*
Rolling in the mud   *them over each other)*
Just rolling in the mud.

Four little chicks   *(hold up four fingers)*
Pecking at the ground   *(peck at one palm with*
Pecking at the ground   *pointer finger)*
Just pecking at the ground.

Three little dogs   *(hold up three fingers)*
Rolling all around   *(roll hands one over*
Rolling all around   *the other)*
Just rolling all around.

Two little cats   *(hold up two fingers)*
Chasing their tails   *(make circles in the air)*
Chasing their tails
Just chasing their tails.

One mommy duck   *(hold up one finger)*
Taking a bath   *(flap "wings" by tucking hands*
Taking a bath   *under armpits and flapping elbows)*
Just taking a bath.

ADDITIONAL ACTIVITIES

• Make up more verses to the song, using other animals:

Seven bumblebees flying all around . . . Buzz, buzz, buzz
Eight little fish swimming in the sea . . . Splash, splash, splash.
Nine hungry lions stalking in the grass . . . Roar, roar, roar

• Act out the song using finger puppets to represent the animals (or make masks from construction paper for the children to wear). Designate six children to be the cows, five to be pigs, etc. Each animal group sings its own verse, holding up the finger puppets to identify the animal.

This is a play that will involve everyone in the class—or, combine with another class and add even more animals!

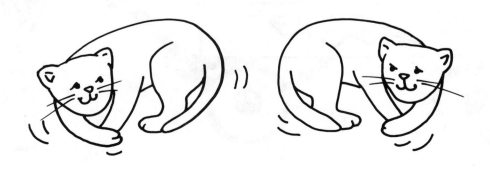

SKIP TO MY LOU
(Little Red Wagon Painted Blue)

Traditional

1. Flies in the butter - milk, what'll I do?
2. Little red wag - on paint - ed blue,

Flies in the butter - milk, what'll I do?
Little red wag - on paint - ed blue,

Flies in the butter - milk, what'll I do?
Little red wag - on paint - ed blue,

Skip to my Lou, my dar - ling.
Skip to my Lou, my dar - ling.

SKILLS: *Matching colors; vocabulary.*

ACTIVITY

Prepare several wagon shapes and matching paint brushes or paint cans for use on a flannel board *(see page 189 for pattern)*. The paint brushes and wagons can be made of flannel or made out of paper and backed with flannel. (If the children are learning their color words, those should also be used as part of this activity.)

Hold up each of the colors of the wagons and review the colors with the children. Name the colors of the paintbrushes. Pass the wagons and brushes to the children. Ask the children holding the wagons to find their color partner with the same color name.

Variation: play or sing the song while the children with wagons and paint brushes look for their color partners. Tell them they must find their partners before the song is over. When they find their partners, they should clasp hands and hold their hands up in the air. Check to make sure all wagons and brushes have found each other.

ADDITIONAL ACTIVITIES

- Let the children color their own wagons.

Make enough wagons for everyone in the class out of white construction paper. Write the color names on slips of white paper to go with each wagon. Make a bulletin board display of the wagons.

Variation: After you've made a display of the colored wagons on the bulletin board, review the colors with the class. Point to each wagon and ask the class to sing about the color you're pointing to.

> Little red wagon painted green . . .
> Little red wagon painted pink . . .
> Little red wagon painted yellow. . .

Test the children's color skills by removing the color names from the bulletin board before you sing the song.

- Sing the *Skip to My Lou* version of the song. Ask the children to help you come up with other words to substitute for "flies" and "buttermilk." Ask them to name other insects and drinks instead. For example:

Bees in the lemonade, what'll I do?
Fireflies in the grape juice, what'll I do?
Ants in the apple cider, what'll I do?

THE LITTLE MICE

Freely

Traditional

1. The old gray cat is sleep - ing,
2. The lit - tle mice are creep - ing,

sleep - ing, sleep - ing, The
creep - ing, creep - ing, The

old gray cat is sleep - ing
lit - tle mice are creep - ing

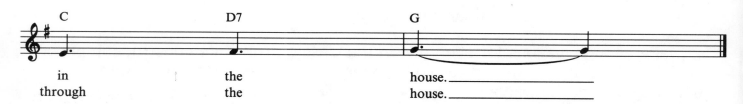

in the house._____
through the house._____

3. The little mice are nibbling . . . in the house

4. The little mice are sleeping . . . in the house

5. The old gray cat comes creeping . . . through the house

6. The little mice all scamper . . . through the house

SKILLS: *Sequencing a story; creative dramatics.*

ACTIVITY

Do the following actions while singing this song.

The old gray cat is sleeping . . . in the house.	*(put head on folded hands as if sleeping)*
The little mice are creeping . . . through the house.	*(walk on tiptoes)*
The little mice are nibbling . . . in the house.	*(put hands to mouth and pretend to nibble)*
The little mice are sleeping . . . in the house.	*(put head on folded hands as if sleeping)*
The old gray cat comes creeping . . . through the house.	*(walk on tiptoes)*
The little mice all scamper . . . through the house.	*(run in place)*

ADDITIONAL ACTIVITIES

• Make several mice masks and one cat mask. Assign one child to be the cat, the rest of the class to be mice. (Or, the teacher can be the cat and the class can be the mice.)

Act out the story—the cat sings the "cat" verses, the mice sing the "mice" verses. Use the above actions while singing.

• Practice loud/soft and slow/fast while singing the song. Sing the "sleeping" verses very softly, the "creeping" verses very slowly, sing the last verse very fast. Make up your own verses.

APRIL FOOL

Words and Music by
JACKIE WEISSMAN and JERRY MALONEY

There's a ghost in the clo-set, A-pril Fool! There's a bear on the play-ground,

A - pril Fool! There's a witch in the kit - chen, A - pril Fool!

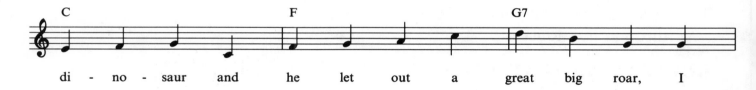

Oh, A - pril Fool! I think I saw a

di - no - saur and he let out a great big roar, I

think I saw a tu - na fish, he waved his fin and threw a kiss! There's a

© 1986 Miss Jackie Music Co.

SKILLS: *Having fun with a silly song.*

ACTIVITY

Explain to the children that the first day of April is known as "April Fool's Day," and that it's a day for having fun and playing jokes on your friends.

Sing the song through softly with the children. Sing the words "April Fool!" very loudly to emphasize the joke.

ADDITIONAL ACTIVITY

• Share some "April Fool's Day" jokes with the class. For example:

What's long and green and slimy?
I don't know, but it's crawling up your back! April Fool!

Knock, knock.
Who's there?
Boo.
Boo who?
You don't have to cry about it!

• Ask the children to share some jokes that they know.

There's a WITCH in the Kitchen!

EASTER BUNNY

Words and Music by
"Miss Jackie" Weissman

Verse 2
If I were a bunny,
I'd tell you what I'd say.
"Howdy, folks, hello to you,
And Happy Easter Day."
Hoppin' along Easter Bunny,
Hoppin' along Easter Bunny,
Hoppin' along Easter Bunny,
Hoppin' along.

SKILLS: *Language development; movement.*

ACTIVITY

Sing the song using body movements or fingerplay. You can hop with your feet, your fingers, your head, your elbow, or other parts of your body. Clap hands or snap fingers during the chorus. In the second verse, first say "howdy" and "hello." Then say hello in other languages (or dialects): "Buenos dias." "Guten tag." "Top o' the morning."

ADDITIONAL ACTIVITIES

• **Creative movement**—Talk about how bunnies hop. Have the children pretend they are bunnies hopping about. Have them hop fast, slow, high, bumpy. Give them vocabulary words related to hopping: graceful, jerky, dreamy, quick.

• **Spatial relations**—Find a large open box that the children can hop into. Play a game of hopping to learn spatial relationships: hop into the box, hop out of the box, hop to the side of the box, hop over the box, hop under the box.

• **Nutrition**—What do rabbits eat? Where do they find their food? Do they cook it? Do they clean it?

• **Creativity**—The verses of the song tell what the bunny will do and say. Create more verses about what the bunny will touch, smell, hear and see.

• **Observation**—If possible, bring a small bunny to the classroom. Let the children observe it and discuss its actions.

WATER IN THE RAIN CLOUDS

Words and Music by
"Miss Jackie" Weissman

SKILLS: *Awareness of water, one of our most valuable natural resources; language skills.*

ACTIVITY

Sing the song through with the children. Change the words to describe water found in other places. Examples:

Water in the faucet—drink drink drinky water
Water in the river—mud mud muddy water
Water in the swimming pool—splish splish splashy water

ADDITIONAL ACTIVITIES

• Talk about water with the children. Ask them to tell you some of the many ways we use water. Some ideas might be for drinking, for cooking, to wash the car, to wash yourself, to swim in, to ride a boat on, to make a fountain.

• Change the words "my my" at the end of each verse to "oh yes," "hurrah," etc. Ask the class for ideas.

HOP LITTLE BUNNY

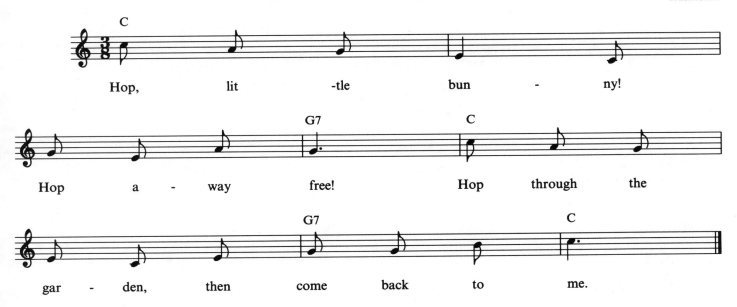

Hop, lit -tle bun - ny! Hop a - way free! Hop through the gar - den, then come back to me.

SKILL: *Gross motor development.*

ACTIVITY

Ask the children to form a line. The "bunny" at the head of the line may decide how the rest of the "bunnies" will move through the garden—jumping, skipping, turning, etc. The "bunnies" follow the leader as everyone sings the song. Change the lead "bunny" each time the song is finished. (An easy way to change leaders is to have the leader go to the back of the line when the song is over.)

ADDITIONAL ACTIVITIES

• Change the verses to adapt to other times of the year.

Roll little pumpkin, roll little pumpkin,
Through the garden, then come back to me.

Prance little reindeer. . . through the snow.

Spin little snowflake . . . in the cold air.

• Do the single-file dance as described above, but tape a cotton ball to the tail end of each "bunny" and let the "bunnies" see how long their tails stay on as they sing the song and do the actions.

OH, JOHN THE RABBIT

Traditional

Oh, John the Rab - bit, Yes ma'am, Got a

might - y hab - it, Yes ma'am, Jum-ping in my gar - den,

Yes ma'am, Cut-ting down my cab - bage, Yes ma'am, My

sweet po - ta - toes, Yes ma'am, My fresh to - ma - toes,

Yes ma'am, And if I live, ___ Yes ma'am, To

see next fall, ___ Yes ma'am, I ain't gon-na have, ___

Yes ma'am, No cot-ton at all, Yes ma'am.

SKILL: *Distinguishing between fruits and vegetables.*

ACTIVITY

Make fruit and vegetable "cards" *(see patterns, pages 190 and 191)*. (Note: to make the cards sturdier, cut pieces of cardboard the same size as the cards and glue them to the backs of the cards.) It's a good idea to laminate the cards so they last longer.

Have the children sit in a circle on the floor. Give each child a fruit or vegetable card. Choose one child to be "John the Rabbit." Give "John" a basket and ask "John" to hop around the circle and pick up all of the *fruit* cards the other children are holding.

Check the basket to make sure only fruit cards are there. Hold up each card and ask the rest of the class to tell you which fruit you're showing them. Repeat the activity, choosing another child to pick up only *vegetable* cards. Let each child have a turn at being "John the Rabbit."

ADDITIONAL ACTIVITIES

Give each child a fruit or vegetable card. Have everyone sit in a circle on the floor.

The teacher sings:

Oh, John the Rabbit,
You've got a funny habit.
You hop around the garden
And eat up all my _____ (fruit/vegetables)

If the teacher sings "vegetables," each child with a vegetable card puts the card in the middle of the circle. If the teacher sings "fruit," each child with a fruit card puts the card in the middle of the circle.

Try changing the words to specific fruits and vegetables, such as "carrot" or "apple."

For an added treat, invite the children to "John the Rabbit's" house for a sample of fresh vegetables or fresh fruit. (You may want to provide a dip for the veggies!)

IF ALL OF THE RAINDROPS . . .

Unknown

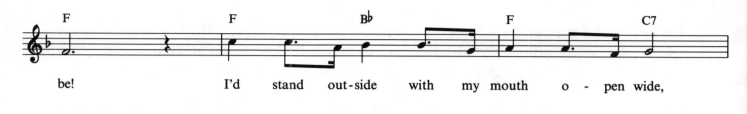

If all of the rain-drops were le-mon drops and gum drops, Oh what a rain it would

be! I'd stand out-side with my mouth o - pen wide,

Uh - uh - uh-uh - uh - uh - uh - uh - uh-uh. If all of the rain - drops were

le - mon drops and gum drops, Oh what a rain it would be!

Verse 2

If all of the snowflakes were Hershey bars and milk shakes,
Oh what a snow it would be!
I'd stand outside with my mouth open wide,
Uh-uh-uh-uh-uh-uh-uh-uh-uh-uh. *(tilt head upward and stick out tongue)*
If all of the snowflakes were Hershey bars and milk shakes,
Oh what a snow it would be!

SKILLS: *Learning about colors; learning about weather.*

ACTIVITY

Bring different colors of lemon drops and gum drops to school to share with the class.

Pass out a handful of candies to each child. Ask them to hold up a candy with the color you ask for. For example, when you say, "Show me a red gum drop," everyone with a red gum drop holds up one. Call out other colors, such as green, yellow, purple, etc.

Let the children eat the candy after the activity. (It's a good idea to have them choose just one to eat and put the rest in sealable plastic sandwich bags that they can take home.)

ADDITIONAL ACTIVITY

• Use this song as an opportunity to talk about weather with the class. What does rain feel like? What does snow feel like? What would rain look/feel like if it really was lemon drops and gum drops? What if snow came down in the form of milk shakes? Would it hurt?

RAIN

Words and Music by
"Miss Jackie" Weissman

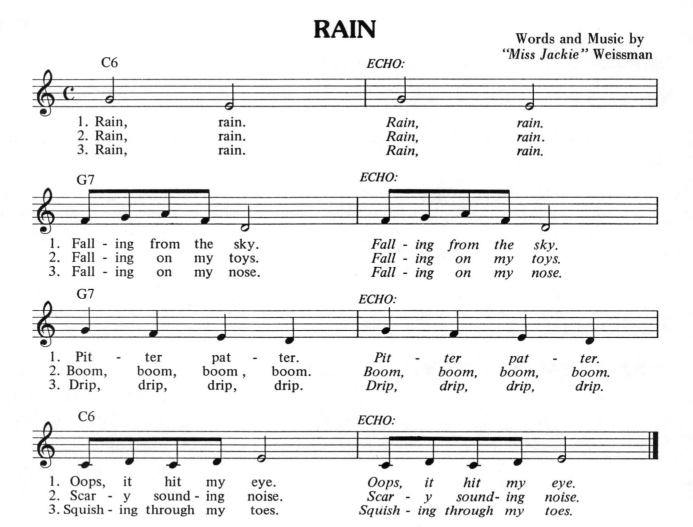

C6 — *ECHO:*

1. Rain, rain.   *Rain, rain.*
2. Rain, rain.   *Rain, rain.*
3. Rain, rain.   *Rain, rain.*

G7 — *ECHO:*

1. Fall - ing from the sky.   *Fall - ing from the sky.*
2. Fall - ing on my toys.   *Fall - ing on my toys.*
3. Fall - ing on my nose.   *Fall - ing on my nose.*

G7 — *ECHO:*

1. Pit - ter pat - ter.   *Pit - ter pat - ter.*
2. Boom, boom, boom, boom.   *Boom, boom, boom, boom.*
3. Drip, drip, drip, drip.   *Drip, drip, drip, drip.*

C6 — *ECHO:*

1. Oops, it hit my eye.   *Oops, it hit my eye.*
2. Scar - y sound - ing noise.   *Scar - y sound- ing noise.*
3. Squish - ing through my toes.   *Squish - ing through my toes.*

SKILLS: *Listening; following directions.*

ACTIVITY

First, teach the song to the children. This is a call-and-response song: the teacher sings one line and the children echo it.

Next, play "The Rain Game," making rain sounds:

Pitter patter *(tap hands gently on knees)*
Rain getting louder *(hit knees harder and faster)*
Thunder *(keep hands going faster and add stomping feet)*
Lightning *(keep feet going and slap hands together to make a cracking sound)*

Do this entire routine before singing the song.

ADDITIONAL ACTIVITIES

• After the children have learned the song, add rhythm instruments and body movements for accompaniment: snap fingers, tap toes, shake hips, tap sticks, hit a drum.

• Discuss rain. Where does it come from? What are thunder and lightning? Are they scary?

• Does rain ever hit you in the eye? Does it hurt? Can it harm you?

THE FARMER IN THE DELL

England

1. The far-mer in the dell,____ The far-mer in the dell,____
Hi! ho! the der-ry oh, The far-mer in the dell.____

SKILLS: *Reinforces classification skills as well as shape, color, number and letter recognition.*

2. The farmer takes a wife . . .
3. The wife takes the child . . .
4. The child takes the nurse . . .
5. The nurse takes the dog . . .
6. The dog takes the cat . . .
7. The cat takes the rat . . .
8. The rat takes the cheese . . .
9. The cheese stands alone . . .

ACTIVITY

Change the words of the song to reinforce the basic food groups.

The farmer in the dell
The farmer in the dell
Hi, ho, the derry oh
The farmer in the dell

The farmer takes a _____ *(fruit, grain, protein, vegetable)*

TEACHER: What did the farmer take?
CHILDREN: A(n) _____ *(apple, wheat, fish, carrot)*

The farmer takes an apple   The farmer takes a carrot
The farmer takes an apple   The farmer takes a carrot
Hi, ho, the derry oh   Hi, ho, the derry oh
The farmer takes an apple   The farmer takes a carrot

The farmer takes some toast
The farmer takes some toast
Hi, ho, the derry oh
The farmer takes some toast

ADDITIONAL ACTIVITIES

- Change the words to reinforce color recognition.

The farmer takes a red . . .

The farmer takes a blue . . .

The farmer takes a purple . . .

- Have an assortment of cards on hand with numbers or letters on them. Hold them in your hand so the class can see what is in each card.

Let each child have a turn at picking a card. Ask the rest of the class, "What did the farmer take?"

The class answers by singing, "The farmer takes a _____ *(five, 'T,' etc.)."*

I'VE GOT A RHYTHM

Words & Music
Miss Jackie Weissman

Leader: I've got a rhy - thm, lis - ten to my rhy - thm

I've got a rhy - thm, can you do it too.

Leader claps four times, stamps four times, makes up own rhythms.

Children imitate leader. This is my rhy - thm, you can do it too.

© 1977 Jackie Weissman
Recorded on *Hello Rhythm*
Miss Jackie Music Co.

SKILLS: *Rhythm development; body movement.*

ACTIVITY

Following the directions in the song, the teacher leads and the children imitate. (Note: if you make up your own rhythms, keep them simple and easy to copy.)

SIMON CLAPS

This is a variation on "Simon Says." Have the children sit in a circle. "Simon" (the teacher) claps a simple rhythmic pattern. Instruct the children to repeat the pattern— but only if you say, "Simon claps."

Use only simple patterns. It's a good idea to count as you clap—and tell the class to count, too.

One	Two	Three	Four
clap	*clap*	*clap*	*clap*

ADDITIONAL ACTIVITY

● **Body rhythms**—Talk with the class about which parts of our bodies can produce rhythms. For example, we can tap a rhythm with our feet, clap with our hands, snap our fingers, etc. Can we make a rhythm with our elbows and knees? Can we wiggle our toes in rhythm? Our noses?

Encourage the children to use their imaginations and practice making rhythms with other parts of their bodies besides their hands and feet.

TODAY IS MAY

Words and Music by
"Miss Jackie" Weissman

1. Sing a song, — to - day is May. —
2. Feel the breeze, — to - day is May. —

1. Hum a - long, — to - day is May. —
2. Touch the trees, — to - day is May. —

All the world — is bright and gay. —

Cel - e - brate this love - ly day.

© 1982 Jackie Weissman
Recorded on *Sniggles, Squirrels and Chicken Pox, Vol. II*
Miss Jackie Music Co.

SKILL: *Listening.*

ACTIVITY

The syncopation of this song lends itself very nicely to the use of rhythm instruments. Triangles, drums, bells and sticks can be used together or separately to play the last note of each line, which is the ideal place to play them.

Vary the way the class sings the song. One way would be to have one child sing "sing a song" and the rest of the class sing "today is May."

ADDITIONAL ACTIVITIES

• Some of the children may not know the word "celebrate," so explain it to the whole class. Talk about things we celebrate: birthdays, holidays, etc.

Why would we celebrate a lovely day? Why do people in different parts of the world celebrate on different days?

• Take the class outside, sing the song and celebrate a lovely day!

DOWN AT THE STATION

Traditional

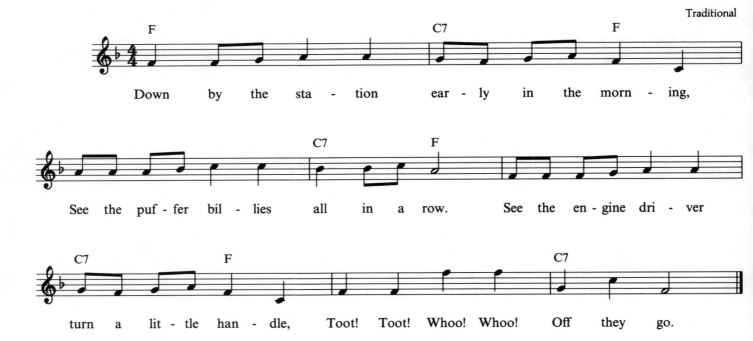

SKILLS: *Developing a sense of rhythm; promoting verbalization.*

ACTIVITY

Sing the song with the following motions.

Down at the station	*(point to the door)*
Early in the morning	
See the pufferbillies all in a row.	*(move arms back and forth)*
See the engine driver turn a little handle	*(pretend to turn a handle)*
Toot! Toot! Whoo! Whoo!	*(raise arm and pretend*
Off they go!	*to pull whistle)*

ADDITIONAL ACTIVITIES

• Have the class sit in a circle on the floor. Pass out sand blocks to each child. (If there are not enough sand blocks to go around, give each child two pieces of sandpaper and ask them to rub the rough sides together.)

Have the children rub the sand blocks together in time to the music as they sing the song. Let one or two children blow a whistle or play bells on "Toot! Toot! Whoo! Whoo!"

• Let the children play the instruments while walking around the room in a train formation. Pass around the whistles or bells so that each child gets a chance to play them.

BANKS OF THE OHIO

Traditional

I asked my friend _____ to take a walk _____
_____ to take a walk _____ just a lit-tle walk. _____
_____ Down be - side _____ where the wa-ters flow
Down by the banks _____ of the O - hi - o. _____

SKILL: *Learning to listen to—and sing back—a melody.*

ACTIVITY

This is an exercise in echoing back a line of poetry or music. The teacher says the first line of the poem and holds the last word while the children echo back the entire line.

Teacher: I asked my friend
Children: I asked my friend
Teacher: To take a walk
Children: To take a walk
Teacher: Down beside
Children: Down beside
Teacher: Where the waters flow
Children: Where the waters flow
Teacher: Down by the banks
Children: Down by the banks
Teacher: Of the O-hi-o
Children: Of the O-hi-o

ADDITIONAL ACTIVITY

• Substitute other words for "walk," such as "run," "skip," "hop," "jump." Have the children suggest other substitute words.

CHE CHE KOOLAY

SKILLS: *Following directions; language skills; learning body parts.*

ACTIVITY

Ask the children to form a large circle around the leader, who stands in the middle of the circle. The leader sings each line and the children repeat after the leader. Do the following motions for each line.

Che-che-koo-lay	*Leader places hands on head*
Che-che-koo-lay	*Children place hands on heads*
Che-che-Ko-fi-sa	*Leader places hands on shoulders*
Che-che-Ko-fi-sa	*Children place hands on shoulders*
Ko-fi sa-lan-ga	*Leader places hands on hips*
Ko-fi sa-lan-ga	*Children place hands on hips*
Ca-ca-shi-lan-ga	*Leader falls to the ground*
Ca-ca-shi-lan-ga	*Children fall to the ground*
Koom-ma-dye-day	*After this line is sung, the leader jumps*
Koom-ma-dye-day	*without warning and tries to tag a child*

At the end of the song, the leader tries to tag one of the children. The children may get up and run when the leader gets up, but not before. The tagged child becomes leader for the next game.

ADDITIONAL ACTIVITIES

• This song is a fun way to help the children identify parts of the body.

Ask the children to sit on the floor in a circle. Sing the song as above, but touch different parts of the body. The children copy the leader's movements. For example:

Che-che-koo-lay	*Leader touches thighs; children copy*
Che-che-Ko-fi-sa	*Leader touches knees; children copy*
Ko-fi sa-lan-ga	*Leader touches shins; children copy*
Ca-ca-shi-lan-ga	*Leader touches ankles; children copy*
Koom-ma-dye-day	*Leader touches feet; children copy*

• This song can also be used to help the children with color, letter or number recognition. The following example is a suggestion for a color recognition game.

Have several different colors of construction paper on hand. Leader holds up a different piece of colored paper on each line; the children point to the same color on an object in the room or on another child's clothing. Or, give the children identical pieces of colored paper to hold up. (Alphabet and numerical flash cards can also be used this way.)

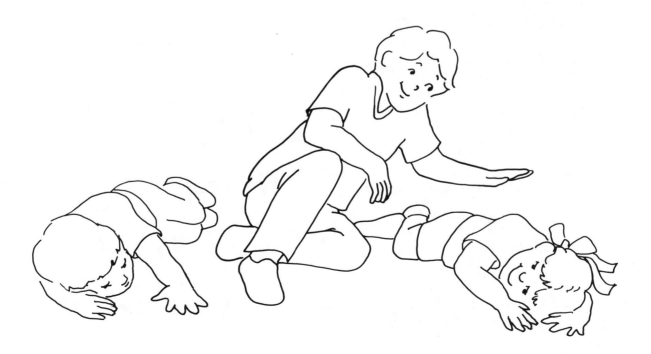

KAGOME
(Japan)

Japanese Folk Song

Ka - go - me, ka - go - me, Ka - go no na - ka no

to - ri wa, I - tsu I - tsu de - ya - ru?

Yo - a - ke no na - n ni, Tsu - ru to Ka - me to

su - bet - ta. U - shi - ro - no sho - men da - a - re?

SKILLS: *Language development; learning a song and game from another country.*

ACTIVITY

"Kagome" comes from the Japanese word for wicker basket. Today, "kagome" means cage (Japanese cages are often made of wicker).

Children stand in a circle, holding hands to form a "cage." "It" stands blindfolded in the center of the circle. As the song is sung, the children walk around the circle. When the song ends, the children stop and "It" has three chances to guess who is standing directly behind "It." If "It" guesses correctly, that child becomes "It." An incorrect guess means "It" stays the same person for another game.

ADDITIONAL ACTIVITIES

• "Kagome" generally means "cage" in the Japanese language. Talk about cages with the class. What is a cage used for? What are cages made of (other than wicker)? What kinds of animals do the children often see in cages at the zoo? Why do they suppose the animals are in cages?

Ask the children if any of them have pets at home who live in cages—i.e., hamsters, fish, birds, etc.

• Like many Japanese songs, *Kagome* uses the pentatonic (five-tone) scale, which is very easy for young children to play. Show the children how to play the song on bells, Orff instruments or the piano.

If you have enough instruments, let half the class play the song while the other half sings it. (Let the children switch parts so everyone gets a chance to play an instrument.)

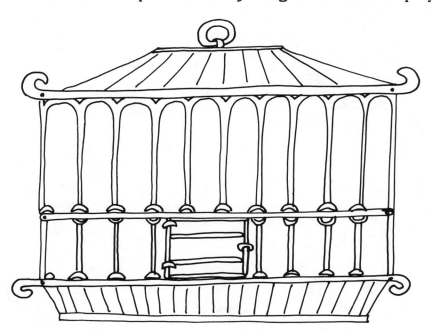

I HAVE A WAGON

Unknown

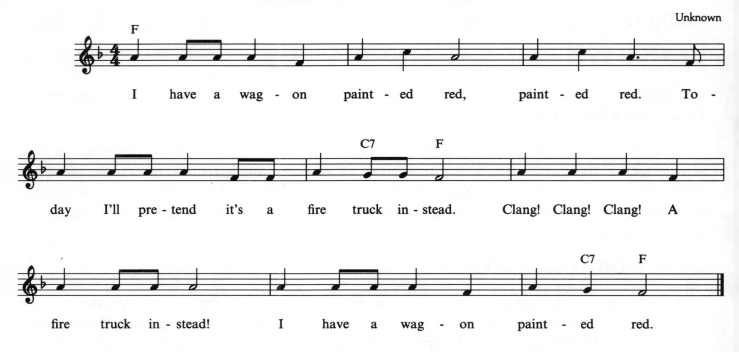

I have a wag-on paint-ed red, paint-ed red. To-
day I'll pre-tend it's a fire truck in-stead. Clang! Clang! Clang! A
fire truck in-stead! I have a wag-on paint-ed red.

I have a wagon painted blue, painted blue.
Today I'll pretend it's an Indian canoe.
Oo-oo-oo in my Indian canoe!
I have a wagon painted blue!

I have a wagon painted green, painted green.
Today I'll pretend it's a submarine.
Bubble, bubble, bubble in my submarine!
I have a wagon painted green!

SKILLS: *Language development; color and shape recognition; learning about different methods of transportation.*

ACTIVITY

As you teach the song to the children, it would be helpful to have pictures of the different vehicles sung about to show the children while they learn the verses. *(See patterns on page 189.)*

Ask the children to help you think of more colors and vehicles so you can make up more verses.

ADDITIONAL ACTIVITY

• Cut squares, rectangles and circles from red, green, blue and yellow construction paper. Put the squares in a square container (a square cake pan or half-gallon milk carton with the sides cut down to form a square cube), the rectangles in a rectangular container (an oblong cake pan or shoebox) and the circles in a round container (a round cake pan or oatmeal box).

Show the differently shaped containers and the shapes inside. Compare the shapes. Pass the containers around the circle and ask the children to take one shape from each container and place it on the floor in front of them.

The teacher sings the song, changing "wagon" to "circle" or "square" or "rectangle." Change "red" to "green" or "blue" or "yellow."

I have a little circle painted blue . . .

Ask the children to hold up the appropriate colored shape.

Variation: Distribute squares of colored paper to the children as they sit in the circle. The teacher sings.

I have a wagon painted *(green/yellow/blue/red)*.

The children hold up the color being sung about.

MISS MARY MACK

Words: Traditional
Music: *Miss Jackie* Weissman

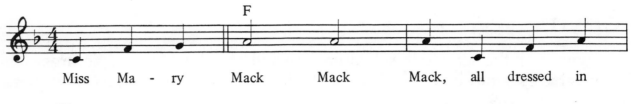

Miss Ma - ry Mack Mack Mack, all dressed in

black black black, with sil - ver buttons buttons

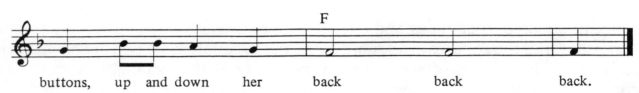

buttons, up and down her back back back.

2. She asked her mother, mother, mother
For fifteen cents, cents, cents
To see the elephants, elephants, elephants
Jump over the fence, fence, fence.

3. They jumped so high, high, high
They reached the sky, sky, sky
And didn't come back, back, back
Till the Fourth of July, July, July.

4. She went upstairs, stairs, stairs
To say her prayers, prayers, prayers.
She came downstairs, stairs, stairs
In her underwears, wears, wears

SKILL: *Listening for a specific rhythm response.*

ACTIVITY

"Miss Mary Mack" is a traditional chant which has been set to music many times. The rhythm of the song seems to have a special appeal for children, and they will respond to the song both verbally and physically.

Teach the song to the children as follows:

1. Say the words slowly to the children.

2. Now, say the first line and let the children say the second line:

   (Teacher) Miss Mary
   (Children) Mack, Mack, Mack

Then, say the third line and have the children say the fourth line:

   (Teacher) All dressed in
   (Children) Black, black, black

3. Go through the entire song in this fashion.

4. Repeat the entire song, singing it this time.

5. Now the children know the song, so reverse the parts: the children sing the first line, teacher sings the second, etc. Then, divide the class into two parts and let them trade lines while singing the song.

ADDITIONAL ACTIVITIES

• Substitute sounds for words. For example: "Miss Mary *clap, clap, clap,* All dressed in *clap, clap, clap.*"

• Use rhythm instruments for the clapping parts. Rhythm sticks, tone blocks or bells will work nicely. Explain to the children how they are going to use the rhythm instruments—hit on floor, shake, etc.

• Accompany each line with movement exercises. For example:

   Miss Mary *(hands in air)*
   Mack, Mack, Mack *(hands touch toes)*
   All dressed in *(hands in air)*
   Black, black, black *(hands touch toes)*

• The variation possibilities are endless with this song. Let the children suggest some.

THIS IS MY RIGHT HAND

Steady Rhythm

Unknown

This is my right hand, I raise it up high,

This is my left hand, I'll touch the sky.

Left hand, right hand, whirl them a - round; Left hand,

right hand, pound, pound, pound.

SKILL: *Learning the concepts of right and left.*

ACTIVITY

The teacher stands with his/her back to the children. Everyone sings the song, doing the following motions.

This is my right hand I raise it up high.	*(everyone raises his or her right hand)*
This is my left hand I'll touch the sky.	*(everyone raises his or her left hand)*
Left hand. Right hand.	*(raise left hand)* *(raise right hand)*
Whirl them around	*(make circles in the air with both arms)*
Left hand. Right hand. Pound, pound, pound.	*(make fists with both hands and pound on both thighs)*

ADDITIONAL ACTIVITIES

• Change the words to "right foot" and "left foot." Instead of "Pound, pound, pound" on the last line, change the words to "Stomp, stomp, stomp" and stomp both feet on the floor.

You can sing about elbows, shoulders, eyes, etc. Ask the children for their suggestions.

• Give each child a piece of paper and two different colors of crayons. Ask them to trace their left hands with one crayon, their right hands with the other.

Help them mark their drawings—"L" for left, "R" for right. Let them try fitting their hands into the correct drawings.

Have the children take their drawings home so they can practice left and right at home.

BLUE BIRD

Traditional

Blue-bird, blue-bird, through my win-dow, Blue-bird, blue-bird, through my win-dow,

Blue - bird, blue - bird, through my win - dow, And sit up on my bed.

SKILLS: *Color recognition; gross motor skills; creative dramatics.*

ACTIVITY

Cut strips of paper (about 2"x11") in pairs of different colors. Give each child an opportunity to pick the color "bird" he or she wants to be.

Pin a paper strip with safety pins to each shoulder to make "wings." Have the class join hands and form a circle with their arms to make "windows."

Sing each verse with a different color of bird. The child with wings of the color being sung about "flies" in and out of the "windows." (Two or three birds may fly at the same time, if two or more children pick the same color.)

Blue bird, blue bird,   *(all blue "birds" fly*
Through my window.   *through the "windows")*
Blue bird, blue bird,
Through my window.
Blue bird, blue bird,
Through my window,
And sit up on my bed.   *(blue "birds" go back to*
                                     their places in the circle)

Red bird, red bird,   *(all red "birds" fly*
Through my window.   *through the "windows")*

Green bird, green bird,   *(all green "birds" fly*
Through my window.   *through the "windows")*

Let the children take their "wings" home to help them remember what they did in school today.

ADDITIONAL ACTIVITY

• Make differently colored birds for use with a flannel board. Give each child a bird. Sing the song with a different color each time. The child with the bird color being sung about puts the bird on the board.

Sing the song until all the birds are on the board.

BABY BUMBLEBEE

To the tune of "Arkansas Traveler"

Traditional

Oh, I'm bring-ing home a ba-by bum-ble-bee, Won't my mom-my be so proud of me, 'Cause I'm bring-ing home a ba-by bum-ble-bee, Buz-zy, buz-zy buz-zy (Spoken) OOOOH, it stung me!

Oh, I'm bringing home a baby rattlesnake.
Won't my mommy shiver and shake?
'Cause I'm bringing home a baby rattlesnake.
Rattle, rattle, rattle—
(Spoken) OOOOH, it bit me!

Oh, I'm bringing home a baby kitty cat.
Won't my mommy be so proud of that?
'Cause I'm bringing home a baby kitty cat.
Kitty, kitty, kitty—
(Spoken) OOOOH, it's a skunk!

Oh, I'm bringing home a baby turtle.
Won't my mommy really pop her girdle?
'Cause I'm bringing home a baby turtle.
Snappy, snappy, snappy—
(Spoken) OOOOH, it bit me!

Oh, I'm bringing home a baby elephant.
Wait 'til mommy sees its great big trunk.
'Cause I'm bringing home a baby elephant.
Rumble, rumble, rumble—
(Spoken) OOOOH, it stepped on me! CRUNCH!

SKILLS: *Learning about animals; language development.*

ACTIVITY

Make flannel board pictures of the animals in the song—bumblebee, turtle, rattlesnake, cat, elephant *(see patterns on pages 188 and 192).* Let each child have a turn at putting the correct picture on the flannel board as each verse is sung.

ADDITIONAL ACTIVITIES

• Discuss the animals in the song with the children. All of these animals are found in the wild.

Ask the children how a pet elephant would differ from a pet dog or cat. What would they feed it? What other special care would it need? What if they had a dinosaur for a pet? a turtle? a rattlesnake?

• Make up more verses to the song using other animals. For example:

> I'm bringing home a baby squirrel.
> Won't my mommy's hair really curl?
> 'Cause I'm bringing home a baby squirrel.
> Nibble, nibble, nibble—
> *(Spoken)* OOOOH, it bit me!

> I'm bringing home a baby timber wolf.
> Won't my mommy go right through the roof?
> 'Cause I'm bringing home a baby timber wolf.
> Howl, howl, howl—
> *(Spoken)* OOOOH, it scratched me!

Ask the children to think of more animals to sing about.

PETER PIPER

Words Traditional
Original Music by *"Miss Jackie"* Weissman

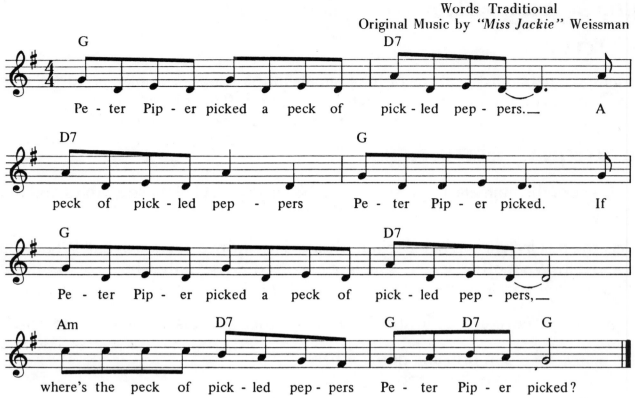

Pe - ter Pip - er picked a peck of pick - led pep - pers.___ A peck of pick - led pep - pers Pe - ter Pip - er picked. If Pe - ter Pip - er picked a peck of pick - led pep - pers,___ where's the peck of pick - led pep - pers Pe - ter Pip - er picked?

© 1982 Jackie Weissman
Recorded on *Sniggles, Squirrels and Chicken Pox, Vol. II*
Miss Jackie Music Co.

SKILLS: *Language development; fun.*

ACTIVITY

Tongue twisters are fun. Young children who are just learning to speak and to read love them because they give them a chance to have fun with words.

Sing the song slowly the first time through, then a little faster, then a little faster, then a lot faster, etc.

Another nice thing is to raise the key one-half step each time you sing the song, again going a little faster each time.

ADDITIONAL ACTIVITIES

- What are some other tongue twisters? Make up some new ones in class.

Take the names of the children and make tongue twisters: "Johnny jumped on Jerry in June," "Silly Sally saw the salty soup," "Mary made a marshmallow malt."

- **Rhythm**—Add hand and body movement.

Peter	Piper	picked a	peck of	pickled	peppers.		
CLAP	CLAP	CLAP	CLAP	STAMP	STAMP	STAMP	STAMP

A peck of	pickled	peppers	Peter	Piper	picked.		
ST	ST	ST	ST	F	F	F	F

CLAP—Clap hands together
STAMP—Stamp feet
ST—Slap thighs
F—Make a fist with each hand and hit them together.

MY HAT IT HAS THREE CORNERS

German Folk Song

SKILLS: *Developing muscle coordination; following directions.*

ACTIVITY

Sing the song through and do the following actions.

> My hat *(touch head on the word "hat")*
> It has three *(hold up three fingers)*
> Corners *(raise your elbow into the air)*
> Three *(hold up three fingers)*
> Corners *(raise your elbow into the air)*
> Has my hat *(touch head)*
> And had it not three *(hold up three fingers)*
> Corners *(touch head)*
> It would not be my hat *(touch head)*

The idea of the song is to sing it first, then begin to substitute actions for the words.

The first time, sing the song through without actions. The second time, do actions for "hat" (and sing the word). The third time, do actions for both "hat" and "three" (and sing the words). The fourth time, do actions for "hat," "three" and "corners" while singing the words.

ADDITIONAL ACTIVITIES

• After the children are comfortable with doing the actions while singing the words, begin to leave out the words and do just the actions. First, leave out "hat," then "hat" and "three," then "hat," "three" and "corners."

• Have a "Hat Day": let the children wear hats to class. Sing the song and change the words to describe each child's hat. For example:

My hat, it's blue and white,
Blue and white is my hat,
And if it were not blue and white
It would not be my hat.

My hat, it has a feather,
A feather has my hat,
And had it not a feather,
It would not be my hat.

Ask the children to make up their own verses about their hats.

THIS OLD MAN

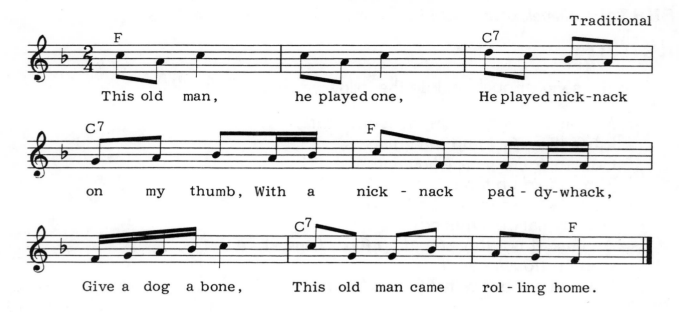

This old man, he played one, He played nick-nack on my thumb, With a nick-nack pad-dy-whack, Give a dog a bone, This old man came rol-ling home.

This is a wonderful spoon-banging song.

On the part that says, "This old man came rolling home," take the child's fists and roll them over each other.

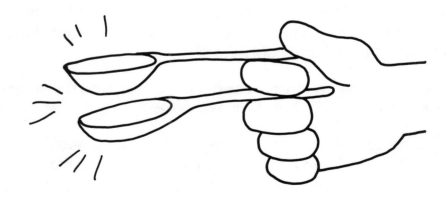

TWO—shoe	FIVE—hive	EIGHT—gate
THREE—knee	SIX—sticks	NINE—spine
FOUR—door	SEVEN—heaven	TEN—once again

It's also fun to do actions to the rhyming word: touch shoe, touch knee, knock on door, etc.

SKILL: *Movement.*

ACTIVITY

Try these new verses of this traditional song. Do all movements while standing in place in the circle.

This old man, he can shake,   *(shake body all over)*
Shake, shake, shake while baking a cake.
Nick, nack, paddy wack, give a dog a bone,
Shaking, shaking all the way home.

This old man, he can kick,   *(kick in place—don't*
Kick, kick, kick, kick just for a trick. . . .   *kick others accidentally)*

This old man, he can twist,   *(twist in place;*
Twist, twist, twist while shaking a fist. . . .   *shake a fist)*

This old man, he can point,   *(point finger in the air)*
Point, point, point all over the joint. . . .

This old man, he can run,   *(run in place)*
Run, run, run, run just for fun. . . .

This old man, he can jump,   *(jump in place)*
Jump, jump, jump, jump over a bump. . . .

This old man, he can hop,   *(hop in place)*
Hop, hop, hop, he cannot stop. . . .

This old man, he can wiggle,   *(wiggle in place)*
Wiggle, wiggle, wiggle, and also giggle.
Nick, nack, paddy wack, give a dog a bone,
This old man came rolling home.   *(everyone sits down)*

Let the children make up their own verses—what fun rhymes can they come up with?

ADDITIONAL ACTIVITIES

• Give each child a rhythm instrument. Sing the song with the traditional verses. Have only one child play on the first verse, have the next child join in on the second verse. Continue adding children until each is playing an instrument.

• **Variation**— After all the traditional verses have been sung, sing them in reverse order—i.e., "This old man, he played ten . . . This old man, he played nine," etc. Instead of *adding* an instrument each time, have the children stop playing, one by one, until only one child is left playing, on "This old man, he played one . . ."

CROCODILE SONG

Unknown

She sailed a - way on a bright and sun-ny day on the back of a croc - o - dile. "You

see," said she, "he's as tame as he can be, so I'll float him down the Nile." The

'croc' winked his eye as she waved them all good-bye, wear - ing a hap - py smile. At the

end of the ride, the la - dy was in - side, and the smile on the croc - o - dile.

SKILLS: *Auditory; language.*

ACTIVITY
Do the following hand motions while singing the song.

She sailed away on a bright and sunny day	*(make wave motions with hands)*
On the back of the crocodile.	*(make a crocodile by putting one hand on top of the other)*
"You see," said she, "He's as tame as can be,	*(stroke bottom hand gently with top one)*
So I'll float him down the Nile."	*(make wave motions with hands)*
The croc winked his *eye*	*(wink eye)*
As she waved them all goodbye,	*(wave goodbye)*
Wearing a happy smile.	*(use index fingers to outline smile)*
At the end of the ride, The lady was inside	*(make a fist with one hand and cover it with other hand)*
And the smile on the crocodile.	*(with palms together, open and shut "mouth" of crocodile)*

ADDITIONAL ACTIVITIES

• Find pictures in nature magazines of crocodiles and alligators. Show them to the class. How are the two animals alike? How are they different? What kind of environment do alligators and crocodiles live in?

Both animals belong to the reptile family. What other animals are classified as reptiles?

• When the class knows the song well, sing it to them, leaving out the last word of each line. Have the children supply the missing word.

She sailed away on a bright and sunny _____
On the back of a _____ .
"You see," said she, "He as tame as can _____
So I'll float him down the _____ ."
The croc winked his *eye* as she waved them all _____ ,
Wearing a happy _____ .
At the end of the ride, the lady was _____
And the smile on the _____ .

For a variation, have the children do only the hand motions to fill in the missing words.

FIVE LITTLE DUCKS

Traditional

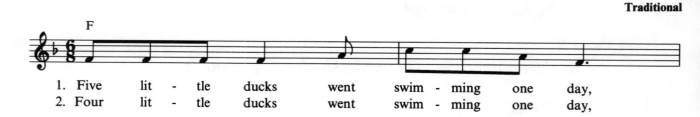

1. Five lit - tle ducks went swim - ming one day,
2. Four lit - tle ducks went swim - ming one day,

o - ver the pond and far a - way. Moth - er duck said, "Quack,
o - ver the pond and far a - way. Moth - er duck said, "Quack,

quack, quack. quack," But on - ly four lit - tle ducks came back.
quack, quack. quack," But on - ly three lit - tle ducks came back.

Verse 3
Three little ducks went swimming one day,
Over the pond and far away.
Mother duck said, "Quack, quack, quack, quack,"
But only two little ducks came back.

Verse 4
Two little ducks went swimming one day,
Over the pond and far away.
Mother duck said, "Quack, quack, quack, quack,"
But only one little duck came back.

Verse 5
One little duck went swimming one day,
Over the pond and far away.
Mother duck said, "Quack, quack, quack, quack,"
But no little ducks came back.

Verse 6
Five little ducks came back one day,
Over the pond and far away.
Mother duck said, "Quack, quack, quack, quack,"
As five little ducks came swimming back.

SKILLS: *Counting; listening; verbal.*

ACTIVITY

Sing the song doing the following motions.

Five little ducks went swimming one day,	*(hold up five fingers)*
Over the pond and far away.	*(make swimming motions away from body)*
Mother duck said, "Quack, quack, quack, quack,"	*(make duck mouth by putting palms together; open and shut them to make "quacks")*
But only four little ducks came back.	*(hold up four fingers)*

Continue the song, holding up as many fingers are there are ducks being sung about.

ADDITIONAL ACTIVITIES

• Make five ducks to use with a flannelboard. Start with all five on the board; have one child remove ducks one at a time as the song continues, until no ducks are left on the board. On the last verse, have each child with a duck put it back on the board.

• Act out the song.

Pick five children to be "ducks." Have them "swim over the pond" by going to the other side of the room. The rest of the class sings the song. When they sing "Quack, quack, quack, quack," have four of the children come back.

Continue until all the ducks are on the other side of the room. When all five ducks come back, have each pick a new "duck" to "swim."

SING YOUR WAY HOME

SKILLS: *Learning transportation methods.*

ACTIVITY

This is a ready-to-use singing game for you and your children to enjoy.

After photocopying the gameboard *(see illustration)*, mount the copy on heavy paper and laminate. Make two sets of the playing cards *(see illustration)* and laminate them. (You are encouraged to make additional playing cards with pictures of different methods of travel to use with the cards provided.) Use any small objects as game pieces (checkers, small colored blocks, miniature toys, etc.)

Turn the stack of playing cards face down. In turn, each player draws a card and sings a song about the method of traveling illustrated. The player may sing a song already known or make up a new song. The player then moves the number of spaces shown on the playing card.

Songs to be used might include *Sailing, Sailing, Over the Bounding Main* (sailboat), *Row, Row, Row Your Boat* (rowboat), *Wheels on the Bus* (bus), *She'll Be Comin' 'Round the Mountain When She Comes* (covered wagon), *Skip to My Lou* (jump rope), *Yankee Doodle* (horse) and *Riding in the Car* (car).

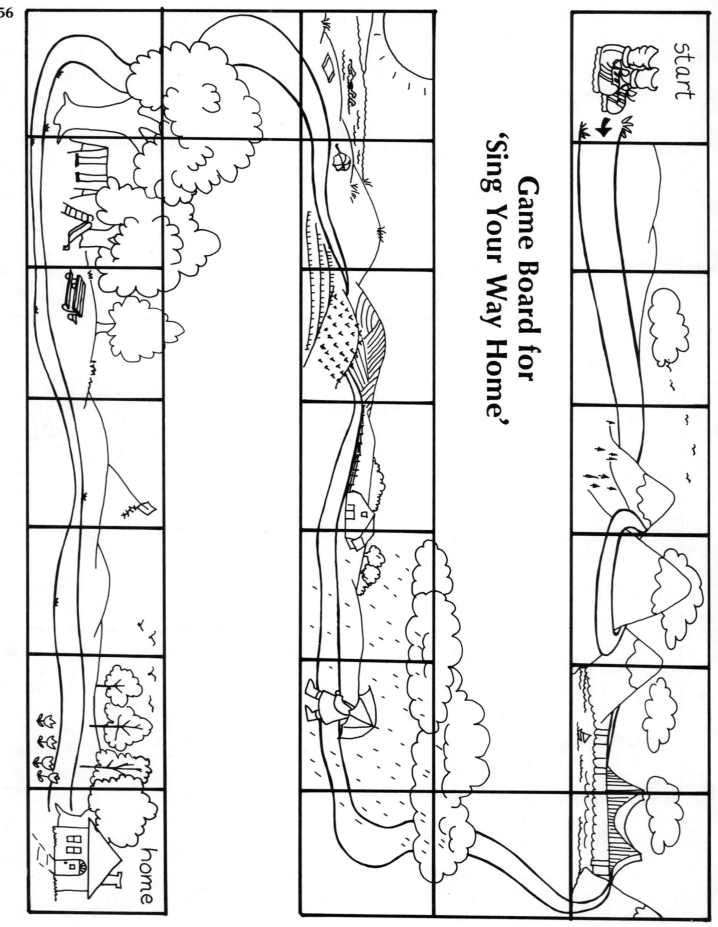

Game Board for
'Sing Your Way Home'

start

home

JOHNNY WORKS WITH ONE HAMMER

Folk Song

1. John - ny works with one ham - mer, One ham - mer,

one ham - mer. John - ny works with

one ham - mer, Then he works with two.

SKILL: *Developing number recognition.*

ACTIVITY

Sing the song with these motions.

Verse 1—Hammer one fist on one knee
Verse 2—Hammer two fists on two knees
Verse 3—Hammer two fists and one foot
Verse 4—Hammer two fists and two feet
Verse 5—Hammer two fists and two feet and nod head
Verse 6—No hammering; pretend to be asleep
Verse 7—Hammer two fists and two feet faster

ADDITIONAL ACTIVITIES

• Choose five children to stand in front of the group and pass out cards number one through five. Line the children up so their numbers run consecutively.

As each verse of the song is sung, the child with the corresponding number holds up that card to accentuate that number. Continue with the remaining verses.

If the children are ready, numbers six through ten may be used, and the verses of the song may be sung to include the additional numbers.

• Pass out five rhythm instruments that sound like hammering. As the first verse is sung, have one child "hammer" in rhythm. On the second verse, another child joins in while the first continues to play.

Each time a new verse is added, another child with an instrument joins in. If there are not enough instruments for everyone, pass them around so each child has a chance to "hammer."

THE ZULU WARRIOR

Traditional

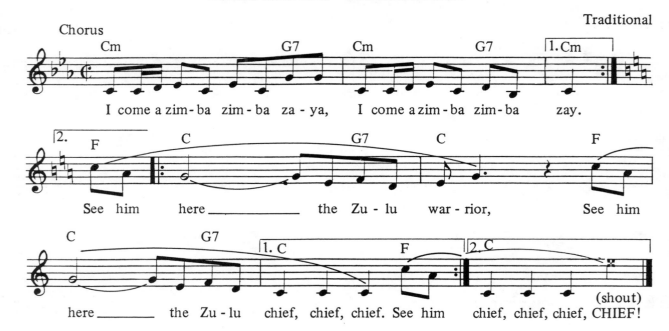

I come a zimba zimba zaya,
I come a zimba zimba zay.
I come a zimba zimba zaya,
I come a zimba zimba zay.

See him here, the Zulu warrior,
See him here, the Zulu chief, chief, chief.
See him here, the Zulu warrior,
See him here, the Zulu chief, chief, chief.

SKILLS: *Developing rhythm in young children; creative movement.*

ACTIVITY

Have the children sit in a circle and sing the song. The teacher can beat a hand drum, if desired; the children can beat their hands or sticks on the floor while they sing.

Choose one child to be the "chief." Have her go into the center of the circle and dance to the music in whatever way she thinks a chief would dance. On "CHIEF!" the child in the circle jumps high in the air as the rest of the class shouts out the word. Let each child have a turn at being the "chief."

ADDITIONAL ACTIVITIES

• With older children, this song can be sung in a two-part round. You can also vary the rhythm expression on the chorus: clap hands, snap fingers or change the sound of your voice. (For example, sing the first two "chiefs" in the last line very softly and shout out the last one.)

• Add rhythm instruments such as conga drums, bongos, maracas, tone blocks, etc. After each time through the song, ask the children to pass the instruments to the child on the right (or left) so that everyone gets a chance to play something different.

MY TOES ARE STARTING TO WIGGLE

Traditional Melody

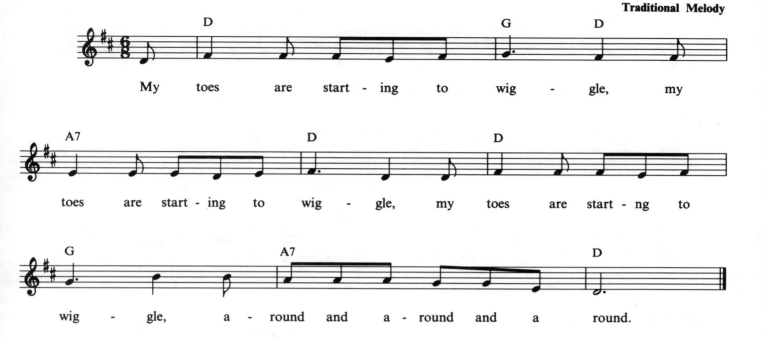

My toes are start - ing to wig - gle, my
toes are start - ing to wig - gle, my toes are start - ng to
wig - gle, a - round and a - round and a round.

SKILLS: *Learning the names of body parts; movement.*

ACTIVITY

The children form a circle to sing this song and move as the song suggests. Encourage the children to suggest parts of the body to sing about.

Additional ideas:

My hands are starting to clap . . .
My feet are starting to stomp . . .
My eyes are starting to blink . . .
My fingers are starting to scratch . . .
My ears are starting to listen . . .

Make up your own verses.

ADDITIONAL ACTIVITY

• Try combining more than one movement while singing "My body is starting to move." Have the children try wiggling their toes and clapping their hands at the same time. Or, have them stomp their feet and clap their hands at the same time. Can they add another movement to those two, such as blinking their eyes?

YANKEE DOODLE

Traditional

SKILLS: *Fine motor; auditory discrimination; language.*

ACTIVITY

Use newspaper, paper and crayons to make paper hat.

Help the children fold the newspaper to make a Yankee Doodle hat *(see sample)*. Pass out feathers cut from construction paper and let the children decorate the feathers and cut the edges (as in sample). Staple them to the hat.

Sing the song while wearing the special hats.

ADDITIONAL ACTIVITIES

• Sing the song through with the children. Sing softly on the first part, loudly on the second. Then switch and sing loudly on the first part and then softly.

• Show the class rhythm instruments. Show each individually, and talk about the kind of sound it makes (loud and soft). Pass out the instruments and again sing the song, dividing the parts into loud and soft. Let the children play the instruments to go with the loudness or softness of the voices.

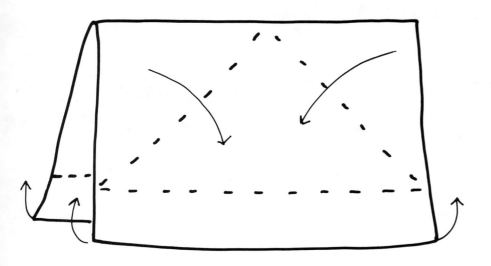

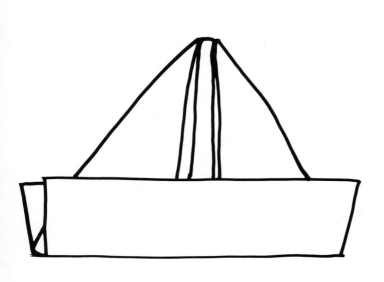

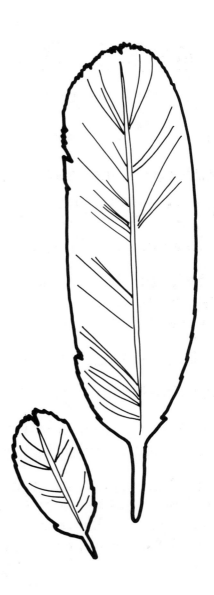

LITTLE SALLY WATER

Jamaican Folk Song

x = hand clap

Lit - tle Sal - ly Wa - ter sprin - kle in the sau - cer. Rise, Sal - ly,

rise an' wipe your weep - ing eyes; Sal - ly, turn to the east; Sal - ly,

turn to the west; Sal - ly, turn to the ver - y one you love the

best. Then you ho - ver up and you pick her up and you put her in a gol - den

room, my dar - ling, Ho - ver up and you pick her up and you put her in a gol - den room.

SKILLS: *Language development; rhythm; creative movement.*

ACTIVITY

Ask the children to stand in a circle and join hands. Have one child stand in the center of the circle and pretend to be "Little Sally Water."

While the other children sing "Rise, Sally, rise," the child in the center slowly stands up, pretends to wipe away tears, turns to one side and then the other, and chooses a partner out of the circle.

The partners join hand and walk around in a circle together. The new partner is left in the circle and then becomes the new "Sally."

ADDITIONAL ACTIVITY

• The children sit in a circle on the floor. Pass out rhythm sticks to each child and instruct them to put them on the floor in front of them.

Sing through the song, with everyone clapping where indicated in the music. Then, let the children play along on the rhythm sticks instead of clapping.

Try using other instruments for the rhythmic accompaniment—wood blocks, tambourines, maracas, etc. Let everyone have a turn at playing each instrument.

SWIMMING IN THE POOL

Words and Music by
JERRY MALONEY

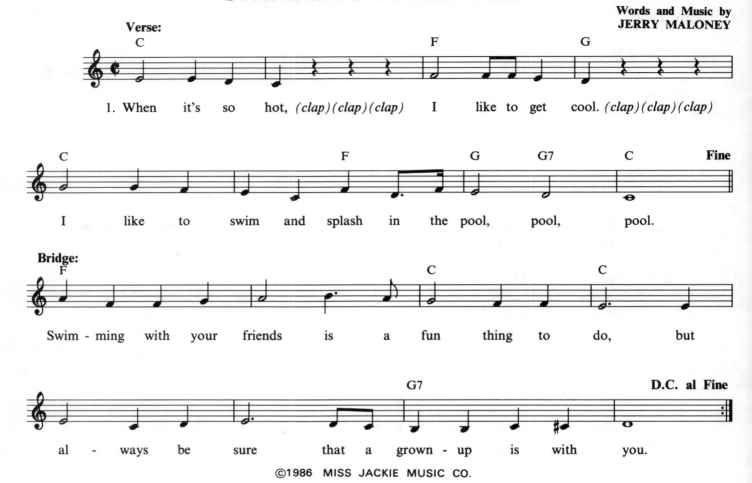

Verse:

1. When it's so hot, *(clap)(clap)(clap)* I like to get cool. *(clap)(clap)(clap)*

I like to swim and splash in the pool, pool, pool.

Bridge:

Swim-ming with your friends is a fun thing to do, but

al-ways be sure that a grown-up is with you.

©1986 MISS JACKIE MUSIC CO.

Verse 2
I swim around. I make a wish.
I like to pretend that I'm a fish, fish, fish.

Verse 3
So when it's hot, go and get cool.
Everybody swim and splash in the pool, pool, pool.

SKILLS: *Learning pool safety; rhythm.*

ACTIVITY

Sing the song with the children. Have them clap their hands or stamp their feet on the silent beats after the phrases "When it's so hot" and "I like to get cool."

When it's so hot *(clap, clap, clap)*
I like to get cool *(stamp, stamp, stamp)*

Let the children march around the room as they sing the song, stamping their feet loudly or clapping their hands on the silent beats.

ADDITIONAL ACTIVITIES

• Talk to the children about water safety. Stress that they should *never* be alone around water, even a shallow back yard plastic pool.

• On a hot day, take the class to a nearby pool. (Make sure there are enough adults to watch the children.) Sing the song on the way to the pool and while swimming.

ALL THE FISH

Adapted
Miss Jackie Weissman

All the fish are swim-ming in the wa - ter,

swim-ming in the wa - ter, swim-ming in the wa - ter, All the fish are

swim-ming in the wa - ter, bub-ble bub-ble bub-ble bub-ble splash.

© 1979 Jackie Weissman
Recorded on *Hello Rhythm*
Miss Jackie Music Co.

SKILLS: *Developing motor skills; having fun.*

ACTIVITY

Teach the song to the class. The children sit in a circle facing one another, put their hands together *(palms flat, touching each other)* and move them around like fish swimming in the water as they sing the song. On the "bubble, bubble" part, the children will naturally become louder and louder until "SPLASH!" as they "splash" one another.

A variation on this is to have the children get on their tummies and pretend to swim.

ADDITIONAL ACTIVITIES

• Make up a new verse—for example, "All the ducks are quacking in the water." Have the children do a "duck walk" as they sing—instead of "bubble, bubble," they "quack, quack."

Try using "All the frogs are hopping in the grass." The children hop like frogs and at the end say, "ribbit, ribbit."

• Another verse could be "All the birds are flying in the air." The children "fly" around the room and at the end say, "cheep, cheep."

• Ask the children for other kinds of animals sounds, and use them in the song.

SIX LITTLE DUCKS

Folk Song

1. Six lit-tle ducks that I once knew, Fat ones, skin-ny ones, fair ones, too.

Chorus

But the one lit-tle duck with a feath-er in his back,

He led the oth-ers with a quack, quack, quack, Quack, quack, quack,

quack, quack, quack, He led the oth-ers with a quack, quack, quack.

SKILLS: *Number concepts; language development; listening.*

ACTIVITY

Ask a child to select a number from one to six to place on a flannel board. Ask another child to place that number of ducks *(see pattern on page 189)* on the flannel board.

Pick out the same number of children to be "ducks" and have them waddle and quack down to the "river" (the other side of the room). Repeat until all of the children have waddled to the "river," then have all the ducks waddle back again.

ADDITIONAL ACTIVITIES

• Change the words of the song to teach colors.

Six little ducks that I once knew,
Blue ones, brown ones, red ones, too. . . .

Make ducks of different colors to go on the flannel board.

• On a nice day, arrange a trip to a local park that has a duck pond so the children can observe real ducks in their habitats. Check ahead of time as to whether feeding the ducks is allowed; if so, take along some bread crumbs for the children to feed to the birds.

Ask the children questions about the ducks. What are they doing? What do they eat? Do they swim fast or slow? How do they move about on land?

BUMP DITY BUMP

Words & Music
Miss Jackie Weissman

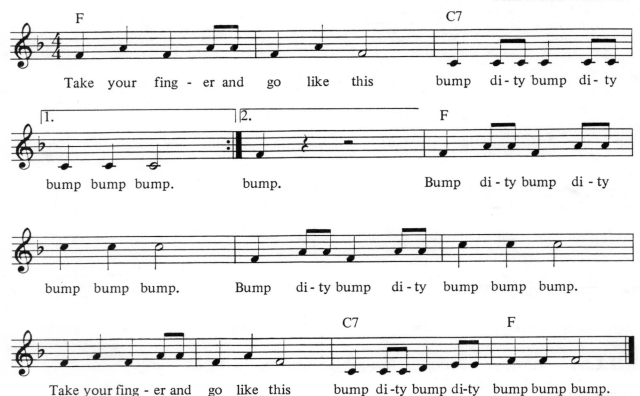

F

Take your fing - er and go like this bump di - ty bump di - ty

C7

1. bump bump bump. 2. bump.

Bump di - ty bump di - ty

F

bump bump bump. Bump di - ty bump di - ty bump bump bump.

Take your fing - er and go like this bump di - ty bump di - ty bump bump bump.

C7   F

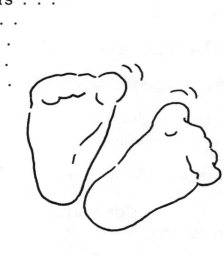

2. Take your hands . . .
3. Take your shoulders . . .
4. Take your arms . . .
5. Take your hips . . .
6. Take your legs . . .
7. Take your toes . . .

SKILL: *Rhythm response.*

ACTIVITY

The children sit in a circle. The teacher tells them they are going to learn a new rhythm: "bump dity bump."

Teacher leads the class in saying "bump dity bump" over and over again. Keep saying the words without stopping and keep a steady rhythm going:

Bump dity bump   Bump dity bump   Bump dity bump

After the children have learned this rhythm, practice tapping on the floor while you say the words. Then practice tapping out the rhythm without saying the words.

Add a new part to the rhythm. (Be sure to tell the children this is an addition to the regular rhythm.) Say, "Bump dity bump dity bump bump bump." Accent the *bump* words—*bump* dity *bump* dity *bump bump bump.*

Now, teach the children the song:

Take your finger and go like this	*(wiggle finger in air)*
Bump dity bump dity bump bump bump	
Take your finger and go like this	*(wiggle finger in air)*
Bump dity bump dity bump bump bump	
Bump dity bump dity bump bump bump	
Bump dity bump dity bump bump bump	
Take your finger and go like this	*(wiggle finger in air)*
Bump dity bump dity bump bump bump.	

After the children have learned the song, it's time to tap out the rhythm without singing the song. Say, "bump dity bump dity bump bump bump," first with your finger, now with your voice.

This is a great song for loosening up the class and relieving tension. Try it just before lunch or recess.

ADDITIONAL ACTIVITY

• It's fun to "bump dity bump" on different parts of the body—your head, your knees, etc. Children also enjoy playing this game with a partner. They can "bump dity bump" on each other.

TWINKLE, TWINKLE, LITTLE STAR

Traditional

SKILLS: *Listening; body control.*

ACTIVITY

Play the song on the autoharp or piano, or beat the rhythm on a drum. Ask the class to jump to the seven beats of the song and then freeze (or pretend to be a statue) during the pause. (The teacher should stop playing at the end of each phrase.)

TWINK-LE,	TWINK-LE,	LIT-	TLE	STAR	(FREEZE)
jump	*jump*	*jump*	*jump*	*jump*	*jump*	*jump*

HOW	I	WON-	DER	WHAT	YOU	ARE	(FREEZE)
jump	*jump*	*jump*	*jump*	*jump*	*jump*	*jump*

The children should stand perfectly still during the pauses. Ideas of statues the children might pretend to be include a baseball player holding a bat, the Statue of Liberty holding the torch, a ballet dancer, a parent holding a baby, a cowboy on a horse.

Play the song at fast and slow speeds and vary the length of the pauses.

ADDITIONAL ACTIVITY

• Give each child a rhythm instrument and have the children sit in a circle on the floor.

Have the class sing the song. Instruct the children to play their instruments *only* during the pauses. (When you begin to sing the next phrase, they must stop playing their instruments.)

Pass around the instruments so everyone gets a chance to play something different.

ROLL OVER

Traditional

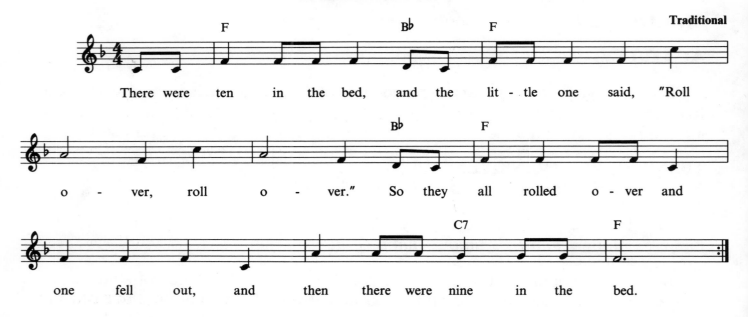

There were ten in the bed, and the lit - tle one said, "Roll o - ver, roll o - ver." So they all rolled o - ver and one fell out, and then there were nine in the bed.

2. There were nine in the bed . . .
3. There were eight in the bed . . .
4. There were seven in the bed . . .
5. There were six in the bed . . .
6. There were five in the bed . . .

7. There were four in the bed . . .
8. There were three in the bed . . .
9. There were two in the bed . . .
10. There was one in the bed . . .

ACTIVITY

Play the game exactly as it is in the song.

Select ten children to lie on the floor (the "bed"). Sing the song and have the children roll over (just as the song says). On "one fell out," one child gets up.

Have the class count how many children are left, then sing the song again. Continue until everyone is gone from the "bed."

ADDITIONAL ACTIVITY

• Make six beds using the small bed pattern. Draw happy faces to show the number of children in each bed.

Make number cards (0 to 9) to fit in the library-card pocket. (Be sure to make the corresponding number of dots on the back of the cards for self-checking.)

Count the number of children in each bed. Find the number card that shows how many are in the bed. Put the card in front of the bed. Check answers by counting the dots on the back of the number card.

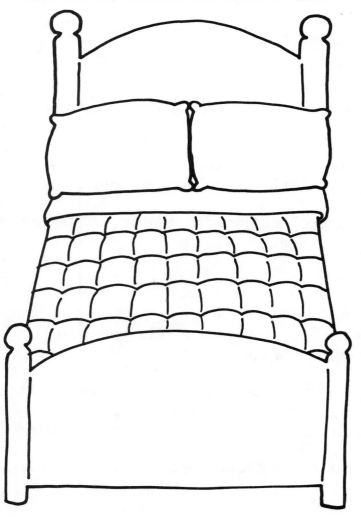

Make your game colorful!

Number cards

(Library pocket cut in half to hold number cards.)

THE CLOWN

Unknown

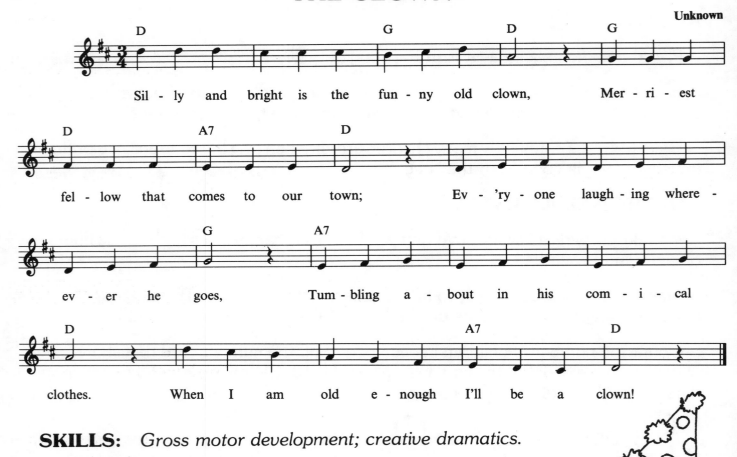

Sil - ly and bright is the fun - ny old clown, Mer - ri - est

fel - low that comes to our town; Ev - 'ry - one laugh - ing where -

ev - er he goes, Tum - bling a - bout in his com - i - cal

clothes. When I am old e - nough I'll be a clown!

SKILLS: *Gross motor development; creative dramatics.*

ACTIVITY

Sing the song, then talk about the circus. What kinds of things can be seen at the circus?

After singing the song, have the children pretend to be clowns. (If possible, bring to school some old baggy clothes they can dress up in, as well as some funny hats.)

Have the children pantomime clowns—juggle, act like a baby, laugh, cry, be sad, sleepy, grouchy, play a trick, make someone laugh.

ADDITIONAL ACTIVITIES

• If tumbling mats are available, provide them for the children to tumble like clowns. (The teacher should act as "spotter" to make sure no one gets hurt.) To ensure safety, let the children have their turns just one or two at a time.

• Make two circles of children—one circle faces in and the other faces out so each child has a partner. Designate one circle the "mirror." The other circle makes funny faces, which the mirrors must imitate. Switch and let the other circle be the mirror.

Variation: Try making your partner laugh without touching or making any noise.

ONE ELEPHANT

Unknown

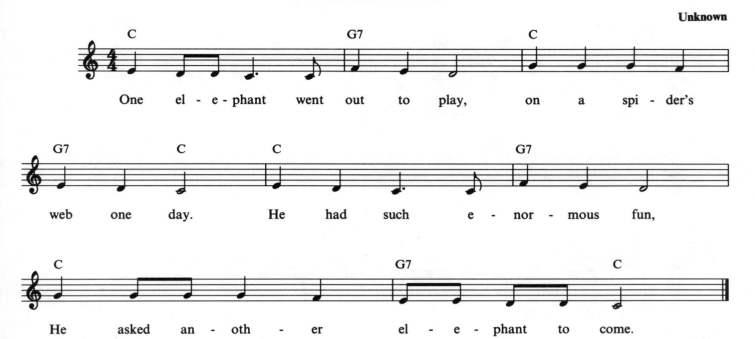

One el-e-phant went out to play, on a spi-der's web one day. He had such e-nor-mous fun, He asked an-oth-er el-e-phant to come.

SKILLS: *Color, number and letter recognition; visual discrimination.*

ACTIVITY

Cut color-matched pairs of elephants from construction paper *(see pattern on page 192)*. Keep one elephant of each color and hand out the rest to the children.

Hold up one of the elephants you kept and ask the child with the elephant of the same color to hold up that elephant. Ask the rest of the class to tell you the name of the color.

Change the words of the song to reinforce the color concept.

A green elephant went out to play on a spider's web one day.
He had such enormous fun, he asked another green elephant to come.

ADDITIONAL ACTIVITIES

• Substitute numbers or letters for colors. Ask the children to match their lettered or numbered elephant to the one you hold up.

• Cut out elephant pairs from wrapping paper, wallpaper or fabric scraps. Ask the children to look for patterns that match.

• Make a circus train from shoeboxes to display each of the above elephant activities. Use identical stickers on the back of each pair of elephants so the children can check themselves.

JOIN IN THE GAME

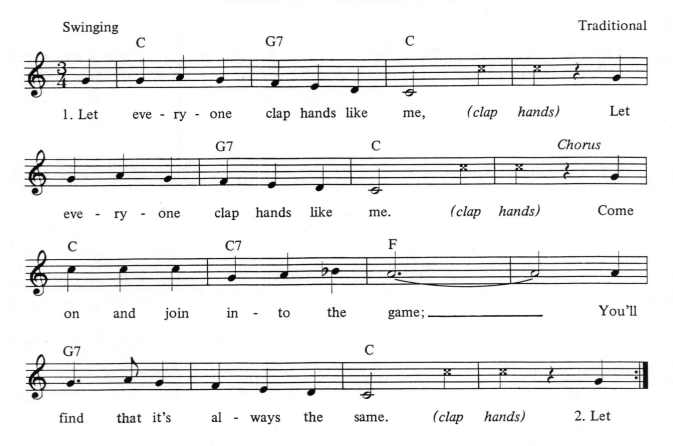

Swinging | Traditional

1. Let eve-ry-one clap hands like me, *(clap hands)* Let

eve-ry-one clap hands like me. *(clap hands)* Come

on and join in-to the game; _____ You'll

find that it's al-ways the same. *(clap hands)* 2. Let

Recorded on *Lollipops and Spaghetti*
Miss Jackie Music Co.

Verse 2
Let everyone whistle like me *(whistle)*
Let everyone whistle like me *(whistle)*
Come on and join into the game;
You'll find that it's always the same *(whistle)*

Verse 3
Let everyone laugh like me *(laugh)*

Verse 4
Let everyone sneeze like me *(sneeze)*

Verse 5
Let everyone yawn like me *(yawn)*

SKILLS: *Listening; following directions.*

ACTIVITY

Pass out several rhythm instruments to the children. Make sure each child has an instrument. Go around the circle and have each child "practice" playing that instrument so the class becomes familiar with the sound of each.

The teacher sings the song to the children, changing the words to correspond with a particular instrument sound. For example:

Let's all tap woodblocks like me
(all children with woodblocks tap their instruments)

Let's all shake tambourines like me
(all children with tambourines shake their instruments)

Sing the song until everyone has a chance to play the instruments. Then, sing a verse for everyone to play.

Let's all play like me
(all children play their instruments)

ADDITIONAL ACTIVITY

• Sing the song with the original words, but have the children pantomime the actions instead of making any noise. For example: instead of actually clapping their hands, have the children pretend to clap, without hitting their hands together. At the end of the song, the children may yawn and fall asleep on the floor.

LOOBY LOO

Here we dance Loo - by - Loo,____ Here we dance Loo - by - Light,____

Here we dance Loo - by - Loo,____ All on a Sat - ur - day night.____ night.____

I put my right hand in,_____ I put my right hand out,_____ I

give my hand a shake, shake, shake, And turn my - self a - bout. Oh,

SKILLS: *Gross motor skills; learning the concepts of left and right.*

ACTIVITY

Follow the song's directions. On "Here we dance Looby Loo," hold hands and walk around in a circle.

Additional Words

I put my left hand in . . .
I put my right foot in . . .
I put my left foot in . . .
I put both hands in . . .

I put both feet in . . .
I put my head way in . . .
I put my whole self in . . .

ADDITIONAL ACTIVITIES

• Use wrist bells on the right hand to help the child remember right and left. (This also adds an extra element of fun to the song!)

• Introduce the song by telling a short story about a little girl who was going to take a bath but found the water was too hot.

RIGHT HAND UP

Traditional Melody

Right hand up and I don't care;
Right hand up, and I don't care; Right hand up, and
I don't care; My mas-ter's gone a-way.

SKILL: *Learning the concepts of left and right.*

ACTIVITY

Before teaching the song, explain the word "master" to the children. Then, spend a short time talking about left and right hands. Put stickers on the back of the children's right hands to help them remember which is which.

Sing the song three times, doing the following motions on each verse.

Right hand up and I don't care,	*(hold up right hand)*
Right hand up and I don't care,	*(hold up right hand)*
Right hand up and I don't care,	*(hold up right hand)*
My master's gone away.	

Left hand up and I don't care . . .	*(hold up left hand)*
My master's gone away.	

Both hands up and I don't care . . .	*(hold up both hands)*
My master's gone away.	

ADDITIONAL ACTIVITIES

• Expand the right/left concept to include feet, knees, elbows, arms, etc. Substitute other body parts for right and left hands in the song.

• Have the children face each other while they sing the song. Instead of holding up their right or left hands, ask them to touch their right (or left) hands together as they sing. This will help them understand that right and left are reversed when you turn around.

WHERE OH WHERE IS MY FRIEND?
(Sung to the tune of "Paw Paw Patch")

Traditional Melody

Where oh where is my friend?_____ Where oh where is

my friend?_____ Where oh where is my friend?_____

Won't you come and get your hug?

SKILLS: *Learning self-esteem; language development.*

ACTIVITY

Use this song as a greeting or as a beginning-of-the-school-year icebreaker.

Sing the song to each child in the class. Hug each child at the end of his/her verse.

Where oh where is my friend Janie?
Where oh where is my friend Janie?
Where oh where is my friend Janie?
Won't you come and get your hug?   *(Hug child)*

ADDITIONAL ACTIVITIES

• Change the verses to help the children locate other objects around the room.

Where oh where is our big flag? . . .
Way over there against the wall!

• You'll have lots of fun playing this as a color game.

While the teacher sings the song, the children must find something in the room that is the color being sung about. Instruct the children to pick up the object (if possible) or point to it.

Where oh where is the color red? . . .
Please show me where it is.

Children may point to the red stripes on the flag, another child's red shirt, a red crayon, etc. Continue the game using different colors.

Variation: Play the color game, using letters instead. Ask the children to point out the letter in words on the bulletin board, on a book or record, on flash cards, etc.

NO NO NO

Words and Music by
"Miss Jackie" Weissman

yes, & please

1. No No No I like to say No
2. Yes
3. Please

No No No I like to say No No No No No No

No No No No No No No No I like to say No.

ACTIVITY

Children want to say "no" much more often than they are permitted. And, certainly, they don't often get to shake their fingers while saying "no." This song is fun for children to sing because it gives them permission to express themselves. What are other ways to say "no"? (Stamping feet, sticking out tongue, shaking head, making a face.)

Divide the class into two parts and have them face each other across the room. They take turns singing the song and doing the actions at one another. As they sing and shake fingers, they can move in a mock-threatening way toward the silent group.

On the "yes" part of the song, the children can nod their heads "yes" and wave their hands in a "yes" manner.

I'M SO MAD I COULD SCREAM

Words & Music
Miss Jackie Weissman

Recorded on *Peanut Butter, Tarzan and Roosters*
Miss Jackie Music Co.

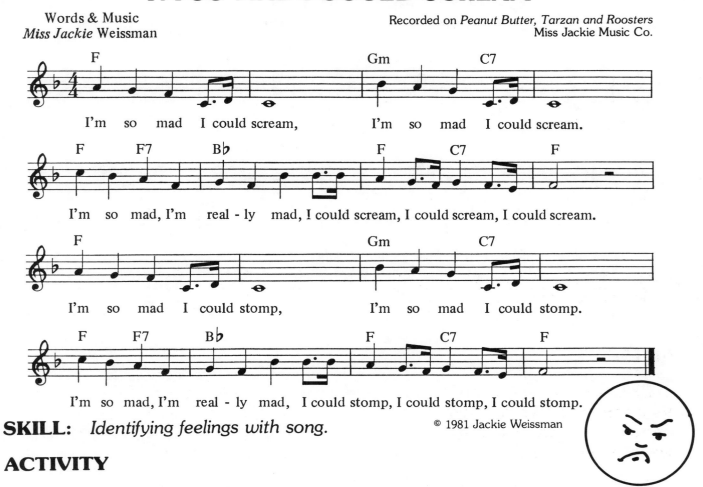

I'm so mad I could scream, I'm so mad I could scream.

I'm so mad, I'm real-ly mad, I could scream, I could scream, I could scream.

I'm so mad I could stomp, I'm so mad I could stomp.

I'm so mad, I'm real-ly mad, I could stomp, I could stomp, I could stomp.

© 1981 Jackie Weissman

SKILL: *Identifying feelings with song.*

ACTIVITY

You would be well advised to prepare the children for this song, since there will be a lot of screaming and you'll want to keep it under control.

Tell the children that when you hold your hand in the air they should scream. When you point your finger toward the floor, they have to stop screaming.

Note: This song is open-ended; you can substitute words to make many, many versions. Try "I'm so scared I could shake" or "I'm so happy I could laugh."

Teacher prepares masks using paper plates or cut circles from heavy paper. Draw the expressions for sad, mad, sleepy, etc., or use pictures from magazines.

One child holds a mask in front of himself, not looking at it. The class gives clues to the emotion shown by relating situations that would make them feel that way. For example: "Heard a loud noise" *(scared)*, "Skinned my knee" *(sad)*, "Heard something silly that made me laugh"*(glad)*, "Got up too early"*(sleepy)*, "Didn't get my way" *(mad)*, "Saw a ghost" *(scream)*.

ADDITIONAL ACTIVITY

• Give the children paper plates and ask them to draw their faces to show how they feel. What causes these feelings? Share ways to deal with anger, fright, sadness.

ALOHA

Words and Music by
"Miss Jackie" Weissman

A - lo - ha, a - lo - ha, a - lo - ha means hel - lo._____ A-

lo - ha, a - lo - ha, a - lo - ha means good - bye._____

INSTRUMENTAL INTERLUDE: *Play or sing* la la la

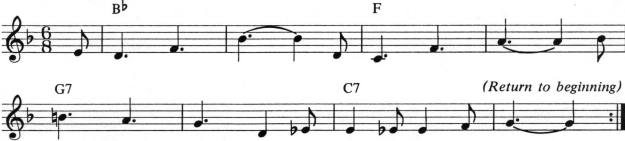

(Return to beginning)

Recorded on *Sniggles, Squirrels and Chicken Pox, Vol. I*
Miss Jackie Music Co.

SKILLS: *Language development; social skills.*

ACTIVITY

Discuss with the children how you can greet someone with "aloha" and how you can say goodbye with "aloha."

Shake hands, wave in different ways, hug and embrace, etc. As you sing the song, let the children use the actions they've chosen with the word "aloha."

This song is nice to sing while standing in a circle. All the children can see each other, and it adds up to a more pleasurable experience.

ADDITIONAL ACTIVITIES

• During the song's interlude, the children can sway their bodies to the music. (If you know someone who can teach "hula" steps, this is the perfect place to do them.)

• Pictures and other visuals would be very helpful in the children's understanding of Hawaii.

188

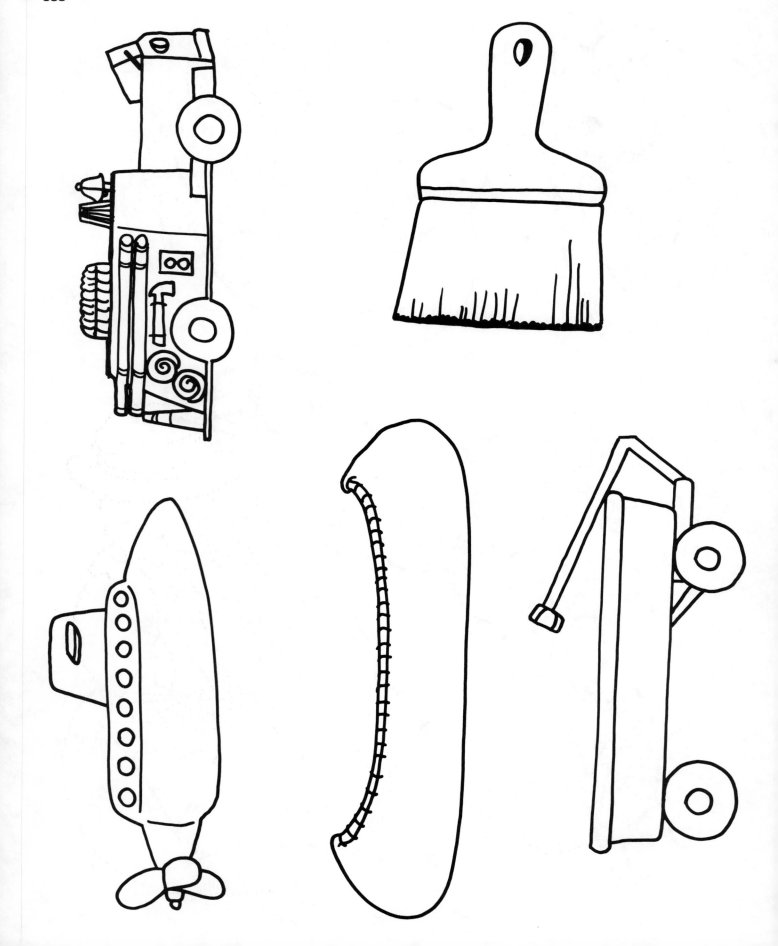

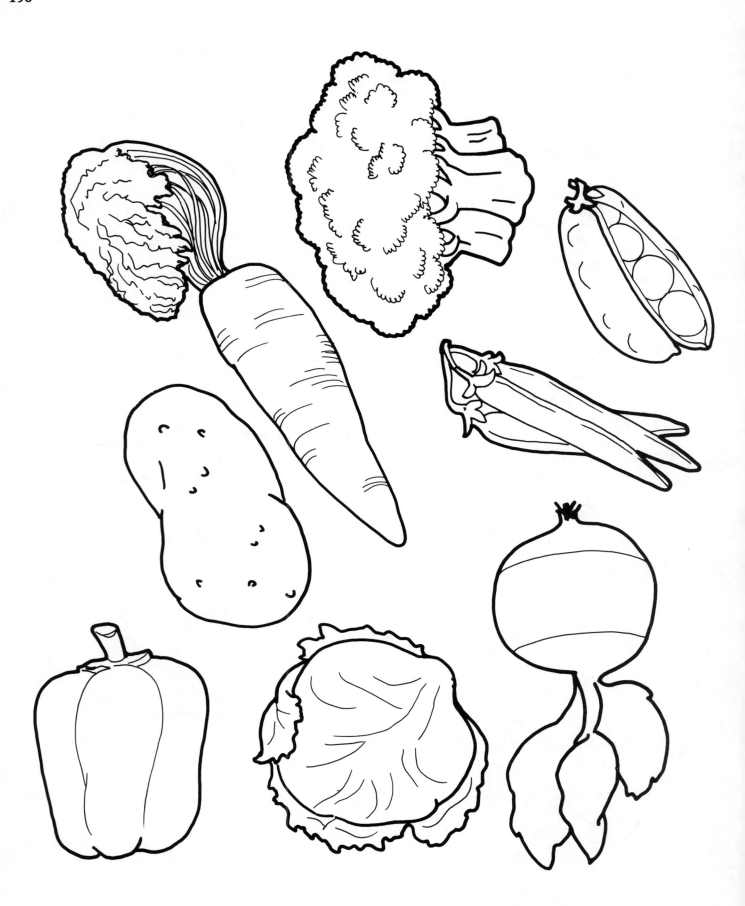

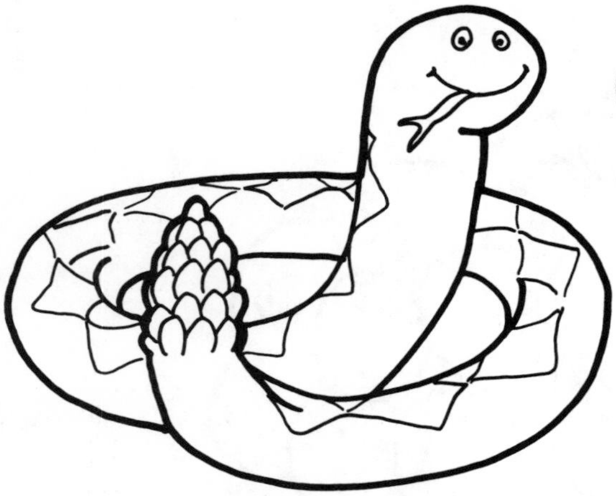

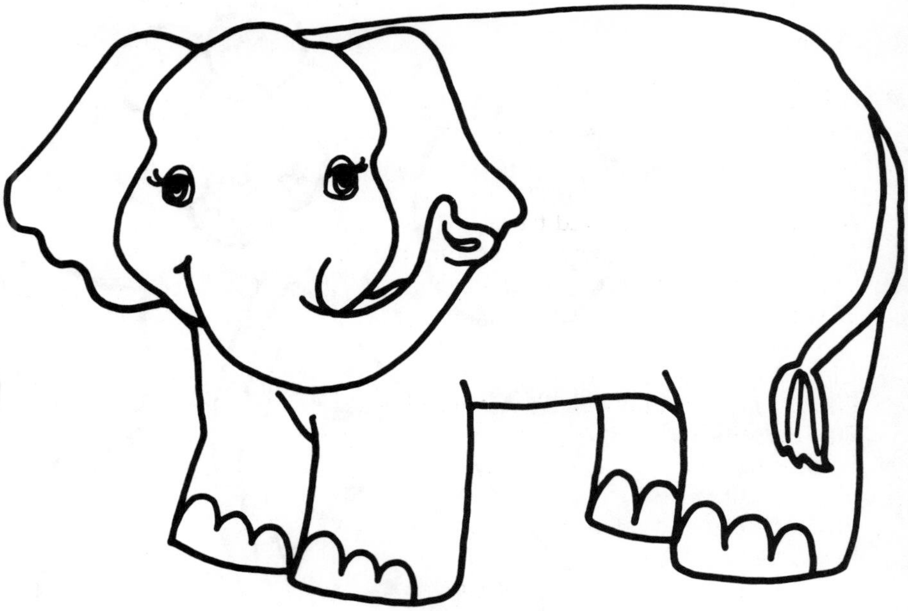

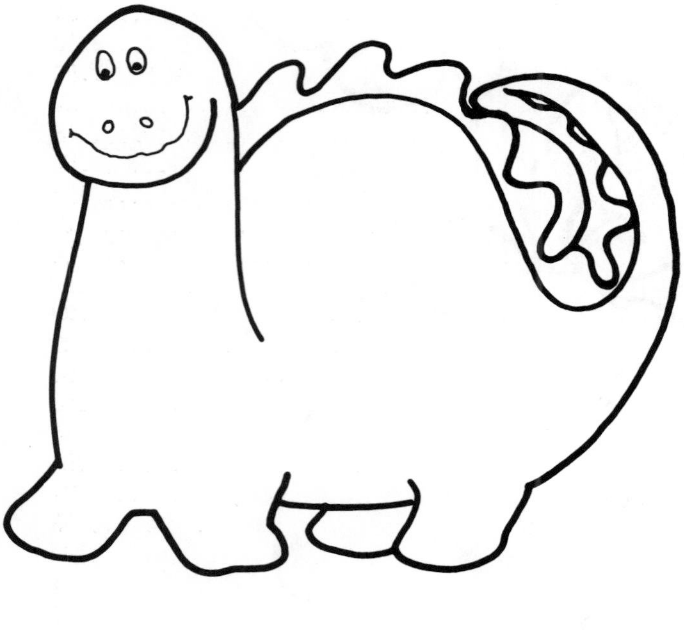

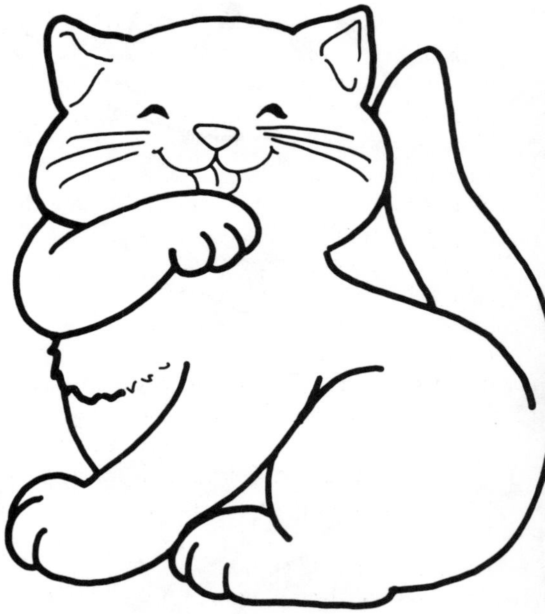

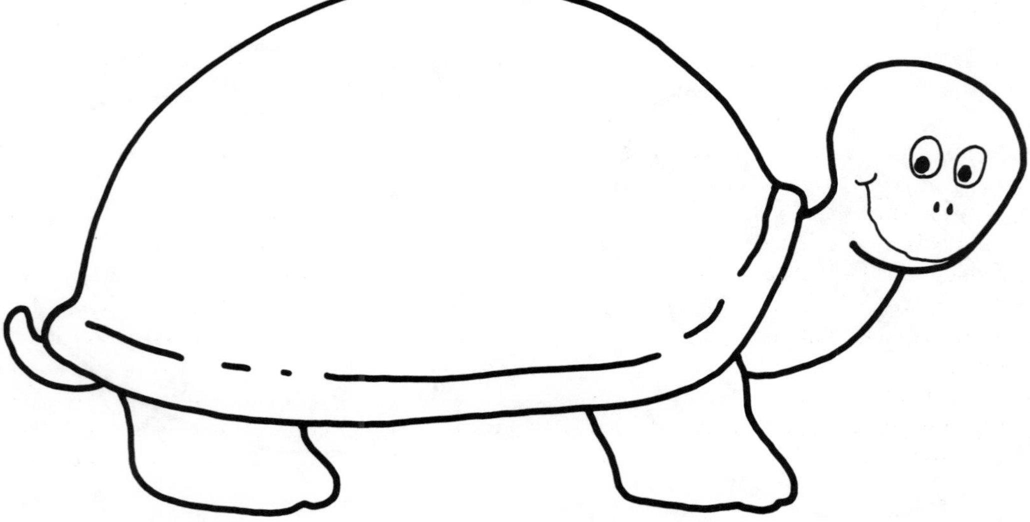

BY FIRST LINES

SONG INDEX
BY FIRST LINES

Miss Jackie Music Co.

— BOOKS —

Great Big Book of Rhythm $12.95
144 pages of ideas using rhythm to teach listening, language, motor and cognitive skills, as well as to strengthen self-concept.

Sniggles, Squirrels and Chicken Pox $8.95
40 delightful songs, words, music and chords, along with activities. (Originally appeared in *The Instructor* magazine.)

Songs to Sing with Babies $8.95
Songs, games and activities for rocking and nursing, cuddling, waking up and dressing baby.

Peanut Butter Activity Book $8.95
Language and movement activities, flannel board patterns, bulletin board ideas and art activities to go with the record of the same name.

Lollipops and Spaghetti Activity Book $8.95
Dozens of teacher-tested ideas to develop skills pack this companion to the best-selling record of the same name.

Hello, Rhythm $6.95
47 easy and fun-to-play rhythm games plus nine songs will expand your child's natural sense of rhythm.

Hello, Sound $6.95
Dozens of ideas and songs help develop reading readiness, listening skills and auditory discrimination.

All About Me/Let's Be Friends Set: $10.00
This book-and-record set includes sensitive photographs to illustrate the words of these picture songbooks that celebrate the joys of friendship, sharing and playing together.

Games to Play with Babies $8.95
Over 100 delightful games for babies from birth through two years of age: learning games, laughing games, bath games and more.

— RECORDS OR TAPES —

Lollipops and Spaghetti *(Recorded live)* $9.95
Valuable learning is mixed with songs that are fun to sing and hear, including "Lollipop Tree" and "On Top of Spaghetti."

Peanut Butter, Tarzan and Roosters *(Recorded live)* $9.95
Songs like "I'm So Mad I Could Scream" teach important fundamentals (such as feelings) and fun.

Sniggles, Squirrels and Chicken Pox, Vol. I $9.95
Recorded in a studio on 24 tracks, this album includes "Baby Bear's Chicken Pox" and many seasonal songs, in a variety of moods and tempos.

Sniggles, Squirrels and Chicken Pox, Vol. II $9.95
Charming songs in many styles of music include wonderful sound effects, along with a variety of instruments and voices.

Sing Around the World *(Recorded live)* $9.95
Children learn songs from several countries and participate vigorously.

Hello, Rhythm $9.95
Self-directed rhythm songs for a child to listen to—and do!—with Miss Jackie.

Songs to Sing with Babies *(Cassette only)* $8.95
Songs are sung in the order they appear in the book of the same name so adult can learn them or baby can listen.

Sing a Jewish Song *(Recorded live)* Set: $9.95
Recorded live in St. Louis for the Jewish Preschool Association, this is a participatory, fun recording.

ABOUT MISS JACKIE

Better known as "Miss Jackie" to thousands of teachers, parents and children throughout the United States and Canada, Jackie Weissman is a children's concert artist, composer, educator, consultant, national columnist, recording artist and television personality.

An adjunct instructor in early childhood education at Emporia (Kansas) State University and a monthly contributor to *The Instructor,* the prestigious magazine for teachers, she is also on the advisory board of *Early Childhood Teacher* magazine, to which she contributes quarterly.

Jackie Weissman is the author of many books dealing with music, games and young children. She has also produced many recordings (mostly her own songs) plus workshops—on both audio and video tape—which are widely used for teacher training.

Music by "Miss Jackie" appears in college texts, elementary music books and learning kits for language, math and social studies. Children perform her music throughout the world.

A frequent keynote speaker at educational conferences, "Miss Jackie" can also be found presenting workshops at many national meetings, as well as presenting concerts for children and their parents.

For a free Miss Jackie Music Company catalog, please write:

MISS JACKIE MUSIC COMPANY
10001 El Monte
Overland Park, Kansas 66207
(913) 381-3672